T0268049

Even If These Tears Disappear Tonight

Misaki Ichijo

YEN
ON
NEW YORK

Even If These Tears Disappear Tonight

Misaki Ichijo

Translation by Winifred Bird
Cover photo by Koichi

This book is a work of fiction. Names, characters, places, and incidents are the product of the author's imagination or are used fictitiously. Any resemblance to actual events, locales, or persons, living or dead, is coincidental.

KONYA, SEKAI KARA KONO NAMIDA GA KIETEMO
©Misaki Ichijo 2022
First published in Japan in 2022 by KADOKAWA CORPORATION, Tokyo.
English translation rights arranged with KADOKAWA CORPORATION, Tokyo through TUTTLE-MORI AGENCY, INC., Tokyo.

English translation © 2023 by Yen Press, LLC

Yen On
150 West 30th Street, 19th Floor
New York, NY 10001

Visit us at yenpress.com ✳ facebook.com/yenpress ✳ twitter.com/yenpress
yenpress.tumblr.com ✳ instagram.com/yenpress

First Yen On Edition: May 2023

Edited by Yen On Editorial: Shella Wu, Maya Deutsch
Designed by Yen Press Design: Wendy Chan

Yen On is an imprint of Yen Press, LLC.
The Yen On name and logo are trademarks of Yen Press, LLC.

The publisher is not responsible for websites (or their content) that are not owned by the publisher.

Library of Congress Control Number: 2022058912

ISBNs: 978-1-9753-6782-4 (hardcover)
       978-1-9753-6783-1 (ebook)

10 9 8 7 6 5 4 3 2 1

LSC-C

Printed in the United States of America

CONTENTS

"I bet you've never had a passionate love affair, Wataya."

It was the end of May when a freshman innocently said that to me. I'd gone to the back of the library where it was shady and cool to escape the warm sunshine of early summer.

The freshman's last name was Naruse, and we'd only met one month ago. He was a year below me at university. Mystifyingly, he had a crush on me. But like every other freshman getting his first taste of freedom, he ran his mouth sometimes. Right now, for example, he was panicking over what he'd blurted out on the spur of the moment.

I'm not the kind of woman to have a "passionate affair."

Naruse is honest, in a good way. I've got short hair and an emotionless face. Add in my blunt personality, and it wasn't a crazy conclusion to draw. Even I don't think I'm the type for it. What does "a passionate love affair" even mean? It's a hackneyed, vague phrase. And how many people our age have experienced something like that?

Still…

"You just don't know me," I said.

If passionate affairs include broken hearts, then I had one in high school.

But no one knows that. The truth is buried deep in my heart. I don't even think the person I felt that way about realized my feelings. Only I know about this heartbreak, this affair.

I checked the time. I needed to go to class, so I said goodbye to Naruse and left.

My answer must have surprised him because his eyes widened briefly.

About two weeks later, he confessed his feelings for me at the university library.

"I...like you."

I was caught slightly off guard, but I had an answer ready. I don't have a desire to date anyone. Now and in the past, there has been only one person of the opposite sex I've ever been romantically interested in. He was an odd character, like me, and we had the same interests. I thought he'd never be able to forget himself and fall in love with another person.

But I was wrong.

Through him, I saw up close how relationships can transform people. As I watched him change, I felt somehow like I was being left behind.

I felt like nothing was beginning for me. Like nothing could begin.

"I'll date you, but under one condition," I said to Naruse.

As you might expect, my softly spoken words faintly echoed in the quiet library.

"You can't fall in love with me. Can you promise me that?"

Naruse looked surprised. But I was even more shocked. I couldn't believe myself. Why did I go and say that?

Was it because he looked slightly like that other guy?

Was it because I wanted to lose myself in a relationship and let it change me?

Or was it that I wanted to forget about that other guy…?

Whatever the reason, I could still play it off as joke if I wanted. I could end it before it started.

But after hesitating for a moment, Naruse faced me and said very clearly, "Yes."

Teach Me
How to Say Goodbye

1

It was the kind of crush where you already knew how it'd end from the start.

It began in my second year of high school. I fell for someone for the first time. The guy was in the same grade as me.

That would have been fine.

People are made to become interested in each other, one way or the other. Anywhere you find humans, you'll find relationships. There's nothing sad or inconvenient about that.

But things were slightly different in my case.

I had a crush on my best friend's boyfriend.

His name was Tooru Kamiya.

He was taller than average, but he wasn't particularly good-looking. He was lanky and pale and used to being alone, and sometimes he looked sad when he smiled. His mother died when he was young, and he lived with his father, an aspiring novelist, in an apartment in a housing development. For different reasons, I also lived in a single-parent household, and while I don't know this for sure, I think he'd given up on certain things and accepted reality, like I had.

I first met him in high school. We weren't in the same class, though. Because of his family situation, Tooru wasn't planning to go to university. Instead, he'd decided to get a municipal job after graduating from high school. My best friend and I were both in the advanced class, which was part of the reason we didn't cross paths with him.

At least, not at first. But one day in late May, a few months after the start of our second year, Tooru told my best friend, Maori Hino, that he liked her.

So there was me, Izumi Wataya.

Tooru Kamiya, who I barely knew.

And my best friend, Maori Hino.

If he hadn't asked Maori out, the three of us would have never ended up meeting. Tooru and I would have been strangers forever. Just simple passersby in life. But meet we did. Each of us with our own peculiarities.

"Excuse me, can I talk to you for a minute?"

I still remember it like it was yesterday. Maori and I were chatting in the hallway after school when Tooru suddenly came up and started talking to Maori.

When I think back on this…I become somewhat sad.

Tooru only had eyes for Maori from the start. Of course he did. She was the one he needed to talk to, not me. I was only the sidekick. Maori's friend, Female Student A.

I probably don't need to tell you what became of Female Student A's crush. She fell for the male lead, that's all. Nothing would come of it, of course. I'm not much for love stories, but in a typical one, my role would have been to make the heroine look good.

I didn't fall for Tooru right away. My initial reaction was a far cry from that. When he came up to Maori, I could tell from his expression that he wasn't excited about it, even though he was the one approaching her. He struck me as having a backbone, but there was something suspicious about him.

Maori agreed to go with him behind the school.

She and I arranged to meet later in front of the school library. I considered secretly watching them, but even best friends need to maintain some basic courtesy. I waited anxiously for her to return.

"I decided to date him," she told me when she arrived at the library. I was shocked.

Maori's genuine personality and pretty face made her popular. And since she didn't flirt with the boys, the girls held no ill will toward her. She was the kind of person everyone liked, but she had always turned down guys who asked her out in the past. This time was different.

"How come?" I asked.

"He asked me out. I thought I'd give it a go."

"I don't understand. Kamiya, was it? Did you tell him about your memory loss?"

"I didn't, and I don't plan to. I thought I could try something new even with my current condition."

Memory loss.

If Maori had still been her old self, I might have taken the news more calmly. But there was a reason I couldn't. Maori had a secret that none of her classmates other than me knew about.

She had amnesia. A particular kind called anterograde amnesia. It posed no major obstacle to her daily life, but ever since that accident during Golden Week in our second year of high school, she'd stopped being able to remember things that happened the day before.

When she went to sleep, her brain would begin to erase her memories of the day instead of processing them, so new memories could never accumulate.

And now she was saying that this guy Tooru, who she didn't even know well, had asked her out, and they had started dating. Later, I learned that she had given Tooru three conditions for her to agree. First, he wasn't allowed to talk to her until after school. Second, when they contacted each other, they would keep it short. And finally…he wasn't allowed to fall in love with her.

2

I might misunderstand a bunch of things and run my mouth a lot, but I did understand that Wataya and I weren't compatible.

Everything about me is average. That goes for the outside as well as the inside. I went through a phase where I worried that it was a problem and tried hard to think of something I excelled at, but all I could come up with was a compliment a teacher once wrote on my elementary school report card: *Naruse never speaks ill of other people.*

I studied hard to get into a national university, but so did everyone else who goes to my university.

I don't have anything unique to offer. I think about that constantly.

But for the first time in my life, I fell in love at first sight.

She was a year ahead of me at the same university. Her name was

Izumi Wataya. I remember the day I met her very well. I doubt I'll forget it as long as I live.

It was April, just after I started school. Under a hazy spring sky, I was on campus talking to an older student who was from my town. We'd gone to junior high and high school together and were in the same club in junior high. He was kind to his underclassmen and was happy I was attending the same university.

"If you meet any cute freshman girls, make sure you introduce me, okay?"

…I mean this in the best way, but he's a very friendly guy.

As we were talking, another student walked by. I noticed she held her head high.

"Hey, Wataya!" my friend called out. The woman stopped. Her short black hair swayed as she turned her beautiful face with its almond-shaped eyes toward us.

That was her.

After, the two of them had chatted for a minute before she waved goodbye and turned to go. But then, maybe because I was staring at her, she shifted her gaze in my direction. I remember the moment our eyes met. Her eyes had a dignified loneliness to them. Deep down inside her was a cool, clear sorrow that resisted any attempt by others to understand it.

For some reason, I sensed that.

But I doubt she remembers our gazes meeting. She turned away and walked off toward someplace for only her to inhabit.

"Hey, Naruse, are you okay?" my friend asked, probably noticing how dazed I looked.

"Oh, uh…yeah."

Of course, part of it had to do with the fact that Wataya was beautiful. But I saw something more than beauty in her. That something was what instantly captured my heart.

"Um, who was that…?" I asked. He told me her full name and that she was in the same department as me.

"Let me guess, you're interested in her?" he asked, amused.

"No…it's just…"

"Leave it to me, buddy," he said.

At the time, I had no idea what I was leaving to him. I smiled vaguely.

About a week later, he invited me to go out drinking. I agreed, figuring it was part of the university experience. A dozen or so second-year students met up at a pub. Wataya was sitting at the table next to mine. I realized with surprise why I'd been invited.

My friend had organized the get-together, and he told me that everyone was just grabbing a meal. I sat down in a corner, constantly aware of Wataya's presence. After a while, my friend returned from talking to various people.

"How's it going? You getting enough to drink?" he asked.

"I'm underage," I answered.

"But you're drinking."

"This is oolong tea."

Seeming to remember why I was there, he smiled, then called out to Wataya.

"Hey, Wataya! I went to high school with this freshman. He says he likes you."

It hadn't even been an hour since the party started, and my crush was already exposed. The people sitting near us shouted gleefully and peered at me with deep interest. As I panicked, Wataya looked over at me.

"Really? Is that true?"

"Um, well, it's just…"

"You should forget about me. I'm a real pain in the ass."

Now that I think about it, that was the first time she took notice of me as an individual.

I was so upset, I can't remember what I said back. My peers pushed me toward her, and we ended up sitting next to each other and striking up a conversation. In contrast to my initial impression that she was gloomy, she turned out to be surprisingly laid-back. She laughed and joked a lot. She was already twenty, and she downed hard liquor as if it were water. I'd even call her cheerful.

I managed to tell her my name, but we didn't get anywhere close to exchanging numbers. I was hoping to talk to her more at the second bar, but she ended up not going. When everyone left the first pub, she headed for the station with a couple of other people.

"Naruse, you better not go home yet," my friend insisted, so I followed them to the second bar. Even though he'd asked me to introduce him to some cute freshmen the other day, he went on and on about some girl he was madly in love with but who had no clue he liked her.

I got home from my first drinking party in the middle of the night, completely exhausted. I took a shower and immediately went to bed… and had a very memorable dream. I was out drinking somewhere again. Wataya was there. She was sitting next to me, laughing, and I turned to her without thinking and asked, "What's so funny?" Even for a dream, it was a pretty rude question. I wondered what made me ask it. Maybe I thought it was odd since she came across as being sad and lonely. Maybe I felt like she was forcing herself to laugh.

She turned to me and said with a gentle smile, "It's better than crying."

I woke with a start. It was morning. Because I made an effort to commit it to memory, my dream stayed with me, and my heart pounded from what I could recall of it.

Humans are strange creatures. It had been nothing more than a dream, but once again, Wataya was there, and I found myself even more interested in her. After that, I pursued every opportunity I could find to talk to her on campus.

"H-hello, Wataya," I stuttered the first time. She was clearly taken aback.

"Aren't you the guy I met the other night? Uh…Naruse, right? The one who said you like me?"

"Yup, that's me. Thanks for talking to me at the party. H-how are you today?"

"Uh…what? Fine, I guess."

It was strange talking to someone who knew I had feelings for them. I felt like clouds of unease and ambiguity were floating all around us.

Wataya's short hair looked great on her. She came off as imposing and cool. But I'd realized at the bar she was approachable once she got talking, with the sadness that I felt from her the first time we'd met seemingly absent.

"Oh, look at the time. I need to get going. Um…bye, Naruse."

I continued to greet her every time I saw her on campus. Our conversations were always about the same topics. Weather. Lectures. Classes in our department. Our mutual friend, the guy from my hometown. But that was enough for me. Wataya was aware of me as an individual. She even called me by my first name.

I felt we weren't at level zero anymore—we progressed to level one, but it hadn't grown into anything more.

No matter what you multiply it by, zero never becomes one. In a sense, there's an infinite space between zero and one.

Level zero was when you were a passerby, part of the scenery. Very often, things end there. Maybe I'm being dramatic, but I felt like there was something between Wataya and me. I tended to that connection with great care. I wanted very much to continue treasuring it.

Once I got used to university life, my biggest motivation for going to campus was getting an opportunity talk to her, even for a minute or two.

"Oh, Wataya!"

"Hi, Naruse. What are you doing here?"

"I hadn't said hello to you today, so I searched for you."

"You're a lot stranger than you look, you know that?"

Sometimes she was out in the open on campus, but other times she was in odd places where no one else went. I was surprised by the area I found her in, and I wondered if she was trying to avoid me because I was annoying, but our mutual friend said she'd always been like that.

"Wataya likes to be by herself," he told me.

He said she stared up at the sky a lot, and read, and wrote in what seemed to be a journal. I'd seen her doing those things, too.

"But when I see her talking to you, she seems kind of entertained. You shouldn't worry so much. Now, let me tell you about the girl I like…"

He started rambling about his great love, but I felt encouraged by his words. I continued to look around for her on campus to talk to her. I'd find her behind the administrative building, or in unused class-rooms, or at a table in the literature section of the library, or in the low-ceilinged dining hall located in a distant corner of the campus, or on a bench behind the library.

"Hello, Wataya."

On this particular day, she was on the bench behind the library. The early summer sun didn't reach back there, and it was cool and shady. She was reading a book.

"Hello," she said. "You know, sometimes, I feel like an elementary school teacher saying hello to their student."

"You'd make a good teacher."

"Should I put on a pair of glasses for you?"

"No, you're good how you are…," I said, smiling. She closed her book. I caught a glimpse of the cover. Unexpectedly, it was a novel that had been adapted into a popular movie. I remembered it because the author was famous for being beautiful. If I recalled correctly, it was an adult romance story by Keiko Nishikawa.

"So you read romance novels? They made a movie out of that one, didn't they?"

"Romance novels? Oh, you mean this? This is literary fiction. Though I guess it would be fun to read just for the love story."

She was a bit more talkative than usual. Maybe she was into litera-ture? I'd seen her in that section of the library.

"Sounds interesting. Maybe I'll buy a copy."

"Go for it. None of the characters are university students, but I think you'd like it. The paperback's out, so you should be able to get it at any bookstore."

The conversation was going unexpectedly well. I couldn't help feeling elated.

"Will it make me cry?"

"Maybe."

"I'm a sucker for stories like that. I have to be careful."

"You do seem like the type who would cry when reading such stories."

She smiled teasingly, which was embarrassing. It was exactly like she said.

"Sorry, sorry. That wasn't an insult," she said. "By the way, did you hear?"

She must have changed the subject to spare me the humiliation. We started talking about our mutual friend, who had finally told his crush that he liked her, only to be rejected. I'd already heard about it. In fact, I probably knew more about it than anyone else. Every time I bumped into my friend on campus, he would go on and on about it, and I was the one who had to comfort him in his darkest moments. When I told that to Wataya, she laughed.

"So you heard about how she turned him down."

"I did indeed. Six times from start to finish."

"That's like watching six movies."

"But every time, to make sure I didn't get bored, he'd change the details a little and amp up his performance. By the time he perfects his story, it'll be a real tearjerker. Or, I should say, a great love story."

As we were talking about love, something occurred to me. I didn't know if Wataya was already seeing someone. Our mutual friend didn't seem to know much, either... Maybe now was my chance to make my move.

I got nervous all of a sudden. But Wataya went on talking, oblivious to my emotional state.

"I'm not sure if he's worried about boring anyone… He's probably just embellishing it for fun."

"You won't catch me complaining about it. There aren't that many great love stories in real life."

"…Yes, I guess you're right."

For some reason, she paused slightly before answering. Maybe because of the pause, I thought I glimpsed a momentary look of sadness on her face, like a flicker of light.

But I was too nervous to pay much attention to that. I could hear my heart pounding. I wanted to know more about her. I wanted to know if she was seeing anyone. I couldn't stop thinking about it.

I mean, look how beautiful she was. She must have been in a relationship before. Had she let that person see a side of herself she never showed the rest of us? Was she still showing it to them? I wanted to know. I wanted to ask her about it somehow.

I decided I'd keep things light and ask her casually. Half-jokingly. As far as that was possible, of course. Like it was natural for our conversation to go there.

"I bet you've never had a passionate love affair, Wataya."

For a second, she looked surprised. I instantly realized I'd said something undeniably rude. I tried to apologize, but she had a distant look in her eyes. Then she smiled quietly.

"You just don't know me," she said.

"What?"

She grinned again. A horribly sad smile. Then she checked the time on her phone.

"It's getting late. I've got to go. See you."

With that, she left. She walked off alone like she always did. Silently, I watched her leave. My heart stood still like a pool of water. She had made me realize that she had a whole world I knew nothing about.

"You just don't know me."

She was right. I knew nothing about her. Nothing about her present and nothing about her past. Bottled-up resentment consumed me.

That wasn't all. Maybe I'd never know anything about her future, either...

Later, I asked some of the other people who had been at the party about her. They didn't know anything about her past, but they did tell me she didn't seem to have dated anyone since starting university. Which meant she must have been talking about when she was in junior high or high school. I took it she wasn't with that person anymore.

After that, I refrained from approaching her. Partly because I felt bad about having been rude to her. More than that, though, I'd started to question whether it was enough to scamper around her like a playful puppy. Would things ever progress between us if I kept acting like that?

Two weeks passed before I unexpectedly ran into her again. It was early June, and I was studying in the library for the exams next month. Feeling worn out, I got up to walk around the library to wake myself up. I made sure to steer clear of the literature stacks. But I ran into her anyway. She was in a study carrel, sleeping with her head on the desk, which was unusual.

My heart started pounding. I remembered how strongly I was attracted to her.

The air-conditioning was cranked up high in the library. I was worried she might catch a cold if she continued to sleep there. I waffled but eventually decided to wake her up.

"…Oh, it's you?" she asked drowsily when I tapped her shoulder. I didn't have any dirty intentions, but I couldn't help noticing her delicate shoulders through her shirt. Unsure how to interact with her, I frowned.

"I'm sorry. They have the air-conditioning on high, so I was worried you'd catch a cold."

"Ah, gotcha. Thanks."

Maybe it was because I hadn't seen her up close for a few weeks, but I couldn't help staring at her. I'd fallen for her hard. She seemed sad but was cheerful, was cheerful but seemed sad… What made her like that? I didn't know if I liked her because I wanted to know the answer or if I wanted to know the answer because I liked her. When I thought about her, my emotions threatened to overflow.

"Um, well…see you," I said. I wanted to talk more, but I didn't want to seem needy, so I turned quietly to leave.

"Hey, I should tell you," she said.

I stopped and turned back around. She was standing up. For some reason, she wore a bitter smile.

"I don't like nice guys."

I didn't know what to say. Maybe my friendliness annoyed her. Was she telling me to give up on going out with her?

"I'm not especially nice, so you don't have to worry," I said.

She was silent.

"Why don't you like nice guys?" I asked without really thinking.

"…They turn my stomach."

"What?"

"Humans are fundamentally self-centered beings. But nice guys don't act like that."

I wondered who she was talking about. She was standing in the library with me. She was part of the present. But she seemed to be staring at some far-off, distant place.

"You don't like them because they don't act self-centered?"

"Right. I want someone who's egocentric, who does what they want without thinking about others. And if possible…I want them to not care that other people hate them. I want them to thrive with that kind of lifestyle."

The way she said it made it sound like an ardent wish. When she was done talking, she stared at me. Then she smiled sadly, like she had that other time.

"I don't think you're that type, so I suggest you…"

Give up? I think that's what she was going to say, but I stopped her midway.

"I…like you."

I felt I had to say it while I still had the opportunity. Once she said "give up," that would be my only option. But I probably wouldn't have been able to do that. Knowing I'd lost my chance, I'd retreat to a lonely corner of the world from which I would watch her adoringly, traipsing around campus in her wake.

It was very easy to imagine myself doing that. At the same time, I knew asking her out was a desperate move. She was out of my league. She'd turn me down. I knew she would.

"I'll date you, but on one condition."

That's why I was so surprised when she said that after a long silence. Maybe I'm imagining this, but I think she was taken aback by her response as well.

"Don't fall in love with me. Can you promise me that?"

The nearly empty library was quiet, with only the soft whir of the air conditioner in the background. In contrast to the outside world, my internal world was incredibly noisy. My heart continued to pound away the seconds of my life.

This beautiful, cheerful, but forlorn woman was standing in front of me. I wanted to know more about her. But she was telling me not to fall in love with her.

What did that mean?

Did she think I was just playing around? That I liked her the same way I'd like a shirt or a pair of pants? But most importantly, what would happen if I rejected her condition? Would she turn the whole thing into a joke and cheerfully end our conversation? If that happened, would I ever get a glimpse of her past or her heart again?

I hesitated only for a moment. Whatever the answer to all those questions was, my mind was made up. I liked her. I wanted to get to know her better. Would my words reach her in time? She might tell me she was joking and withdraw her offer at any moment. *Please, make it in time*, I prayed.

"Yes," I said.

3

Why did Tooru ask Maori out that day in our second year of high school, when he didn't know her and seemed to have no interest in her? I wondered about that for the longest time.

It was a dare I took to protect a friend who was being bullied.

Maybe it's a good thing I didn't find out right away. If I had, I probably would have resented him, because I didn't know what he was really like at that point. I might even have told Maori she should break up with him right away. But Maori seemed to have guessed that it was a dare. It was exactly because she knew he didn't have feelings for her that she was able to say yes and try something new, even with her anterograde amnesia.

In other words, they didn't start dating because they liked each other. Tooru had his reasons, and Maori had hers. Since she started this all on her own, she hid the fact that they weren't a real couple from me. That was part of why I was suspicious about him at first. I even suspected he had an ulterior motive for approaching her. My personality also played a factor. Unlike Maori, I didn't get along with everyone. I was amicable on the surface, but I didn't trust people easily.

I was afraid of people.

Unlike the characters in a novel, real human beings don't always share what they're thinking. The only way to get to know someone is by talking to them or reading their emotions through their face, but words and expressions can easily be faked. That was why I tried not to get close to anyone except for a few specific people. Instead of being popular, I'd figured I would get really close with that small circle of friends.

In high school, that was Maori. She was never two-faced. We had the same class in our first year. She befriended me despite my cold exterior. Before I knew it, we were best friends. I also respected her. She was a hard worker through and through. Sometimes between classes, she would stare at the middle finger of her right hand. I think I was the only one who noticed. She had a callus there from holding a pen. We went to a public college-preparatory high school, and everyone there had done fairly well in junior high. She kept grinding away after she was accepted to make sure she didn't fall behind. That was why her callus never disappeared. I think she used to stare at it to judge her own efforts.

But she was only able to keep working like that until her accident. After she got amnesia, she couldn't study anymore. No matter how much she studied in one day, the information never stuck. The next day, she would forget everything. But she still kept up a positive attitude. Thanks to the national disability policy and the cooperation from the school administrators, all she needed to do to graduate was attend school for a certain number of days. So she kept coming to class, and it was better for her mental health than taking time off or quitting and just sitting at home day in and day out. Inevitably, though, there were times when it was emotionally difficult for her. She would wake up in the morning and learn all over again that she had amnesia. She had to accept that and somehow go on with life every day. Naturally, it wasn't easy. And she didn't always feel the same way.

"There's no point in living like that."

She'd said that once. When she didn't show up at school, I got worried and stopped by her house. She was shut up in her room. I think she'd been crying.

Maori must have felt like she'd been robbed of a future. So long as she had amnesia, she could never build anything up over time. No matter how hard she worked on any given day, everything was reset when she went to sleep at night.

The person who alleviated some of that pain…was Tooru.

Tooru, who wasn't even supposed to like Maori, was able to do what I couldn't do. Even though he was a fake boyfriend, he stuck by her side. And continued to stay there.

Maori's parents and I thought we were supporting her as her family and best friend. But there are things family can't do, things a friend couldn't help with.

But a boyfriend, now, that's different.

I'm going to show tomorrow's Hino a good time.

At some point, Tooru truly fell in love with Maori. It was after he found out about her amnesia that she'd hidden from him.

Maori recorded her daily life in her notebooks and binder, using her diary to keep track of her memories. She wrote good things and bad things in them. Some of the entries made her happy while others made her sad. Tooru figured that out and tried to fill her diary with as many fun things as possible.

He did it in hopes that every morning when Maori was confronted with her anterograde amnesia, her diary would give her courage so that she wouldn't be overcome with hopelessness. He ran himself ragged doing that. But she began to smile naturally when she was next to him.

I observed the two of them silently. I watched on as Tooru was transformed by their relationship, and even Maori, who couldn't form new memories, changed. But maybe that's the wrong way of putting it.

All I could do was watch silently.

I'd read a lot of books up until that point. I thought I understood life. But as obvious as it sounds…books can't replace reality.

4

When I woke up, I thought it was all a dream.

Of course, I didn't really think that. Reality is strong. But it felt unreal enough to have been a dream. I was dating Wataya. I had told her I liked her in the library, and she had accepted my confession, conditionally. Then we exchanged numbers.

"So starting today, we're a couple?" she asked.

"I guess so…"

"How does it feel to be dating an older woman? Does it get you going?"

"Well, um…"

"I'm joking. You don't have to answer that."

She seemed to have forgotten her seriousness of a few minutes ago. Continuing to joke around, she picked up the books spread out on her desk and made to leave.

"Um, Wataya. Why can't I fall in love with you?" I gathered the courage to ask.

She looked back at me, staring directly into my eyes. I continued.

"I might not have conveyed it well, but I really do—"

"Then it's no good. Let's cut things off now."

Her blunt statement frightened me. She thought for a moment.

"It's just that I… A make-believe relationship is enough. I don't care if it's a surface-level thing. I'd actually prefer that. If you don't like the condition I set, then like I said—"

Let's end it.

I interrupted her before she could say that.

"No, it's fine. As long as I can be with you."

Make-believe. She had just called our relationship that.

Surface level is enough.

I thought about how to make sense of that. I arrived at an answer surprisingly quickly. Make-believe was fine. That was all right for now. We could start out by pretending, but maybe at some point, we'd become a real couple.

I thought about that as I got ready to go to class the next morning. When I started university, I got my own apartment near campus. I left earlier than usual that morning because I had a lecture first period. My place was less than a ten-minute walk. As soon as I got on campus, I started looking around for Wataya out of habit.

I could have texted her something like *Hey, are you coming to school today?* But we'd only been dating for a day, so I didn't have the guts. In the end, the morning passed without my seeing her. At lunchtime, I went to the dining hall with some friends in our department. As I was trying to decide what to eat, I saw something out of the corner of my eye. I turned in that direction and saw Wataya carrying her tray of food to a table by herself.

"Staring at Wataya again?" one of my friends joked. They all knew I liked her, which was why they recognized her. They looked in her direction.

"Wow, she seems totally unbothered by eating alone. She's so cool."

"She's a strange one. Aloof or something."

My guess is that everyone at our school thought that way about her. Amid the herds of students who clumped together for fear that people would think they had no friends, she was completely fine with being alone, remaining dignified, cool, and mysterious...

I couldn't believe I was dating her, even with conditions.

I told my friends I was going to get us a table and took out my phone. After hesitating for a moment, I sent her a message.

Hello. I found you.

I was slightly nervous. What would I do if she saw the message but ignored it because it was from me? How would I feel if I saw her do that?

Out of the corner of my eye, I saw her notice my text and pick up her phone. She tapped the screen and peered at it, then started looking around the cafeteria. When she found me, she laughed softly. She typed something, and I received a message.

Your hair is sticking up. You should fix it.

I instinctively brought my hand to my head. As I searched anxiously for the offending patch of hair, another text came.

Sorry, kidding.

I looked over at her. She was gently smiling.

We'd started dating, but that didn't mean our relationship dramatically progressed or regressed. On campus, Wataya acted like she always did, and I didn't cramp her style by staring at her with googly eyes or anything. I didn't tell my friends we were dating, and I don't think she did, either. Still, one thing did change noticeably.

"Hey. Whatcha reading?"

Since the university library was near my apartment, I usually went there to study and read. One day as I was opening the book I'd seen her reading before, she came up to me.

"Come on, it's not that surprising. Your eyes look like they're going to pop out of your head," she added.

She had never approached me before. I must have been gaping like she said.

"I know, but…you caught me off guard."

She smiled and sat down next to me.

"Hey, is that the book we were talking about the other day?" she asked.

"Yup. They had it at the university bookstore, so I got a copy."

"Are you sure you'll be okay reading it here? It would be weird to see someone so openly crying over a novel in the library."

I imagined that scene. Strange indeed.

"No worries; if I feel tears coming on, I'll run to the bathroom," I said.

"That would be even more odd."

She smiled, her chin resting in her hand. Her becomingly short black hair swayed. She was breathtakingly beautiful. As I gazed at her, bedazzled, she asked, "By the way, have you ever had a girlfriend before?"

The question must have been related to our pretend relationship. I wasn't sure how to answer but ultimately decided to be honest, since I didn't have anything to hide.

"Yeah."

"I'm surprised. What was she like?"

"Well, she was good at cooking and housework, and she liked growing up," I said.

I'd been so intent on answering her question that I ended up blurting out something only I could understand. Who would know what "she liked growing up" meant?

"Hmm, good at cooking and housework, and…"

Wataya was confused, of course. I tried to explain. We'd started dating in our first year of high school, and she was my first girlfriend. She was not only generous but blessed with a shapely figure. Elementary school had been okay, but in high school, a hierarchy emerged in class that was determined by appearance, among other things. For some reason, though, she existed outside of that hierarchy. She would voluntarily take the lead in cleaning the classroom, using her mother's secret techniques to get it spick-and-span.

She strode around boldly and smiled cheerfully; everyone adored her like she was some kind of mascot. But she was also much smarter than the other kids. She loved the words *grow up*. She'd eat her large homemade packed lunches and say her dream was to get a job with the Ministry of Agriculture, Forestry and Fisheries to raise Japan's food self-sufficiency rate.

Wataya seemed shocked by this description of my ex-girlfriend.

"But why did you go out with her?" she asked.

"I was skinny, and she used to tell me to eat more and give me rice balls and stuff."

"And?"

"I don't know if the rice was good or if the seaweed was high quality, but those rice balls were amazing."

They were so good, I started to wonder about the other things in her boxed lunches, and she started sharing them with me. Before I knew it, she was making an extra lunch just for me, and I had a crush on her.

Wataya covered her face with her hands. I wondered what she was doing; she was laughing hysterically.

"Seriously, what's up with that? It's too wholesome!"

"It's the truth. She also used to bring me thermoses of green tea, and I don't know what she did, but it was the best tea ever. Like, it was sweet or something. Of course she didn't put sugar in it or anything."

Sadly, we broke up in our third year when the intense studying for university entrance exams began. It was spring. We were having a picnic in the park, eating rice balls and drinking green tea. We hung out for a while, and around sunset, we waved at each other like elementary school kids and said goodbye. Then she strode off alone into the sunset. She always smiled so happily.

But that day, I realized maybe I didn't understand her true self at all. I felt like she had kept it hidden from me. I wondered if I had been drawn to the weakness and loneliness she didn't let show.

I didn't tell Wataya that part. I left the funny story as a funny story. To let her think of my past as happy-go-lucky.

My story must have been entertaining because it put a gentle smile on her face. An expression I had never seen before, that I hadn't discovered until now. That's how natural it looked.

"By the way," I asked her, "did you go out with anyone in junior high or high school?"

Her smile instantly disappeared.

"Not in junior high, I can tell you that."

"Then in high school?"

She gave a sad little grin.

"Maybe."

"You're making me curious."

"I did kiss him once."

"Was it…the person you were head over heels for?"

"So you remember that."

"Of course I do. I've been thinking about it ever since you said it."

She looked at me again and smiled, but she didn't answer my question.

"Well, I think that's enough for today," she said, standing up and walking off.

I watched her familiar back recede. It was the back of someone who has walked through life alone.

5

I learned about Tooru's knack for housework and cooking a couple of days after he and Maori started dating.

After they got together, they would meet in his classroom after school to talk. I joined them that day to get a sense of who he was. Maori suggested that since we were all here, we should get to know one another better, and we ended up going to his house. He lived with his father in a housing complex. Normally, you'd expect a household of two guys to be a mess, but their apartment was shockingly clean.

Tooru was very particular about keeping things not just tidy, but sanitary. You can fake being clean, but you can't fake being sanitary. That's what he told us. I found it amusing that a high school student was so particular about housework but was also strangely moved by it.

"I didn't realize till we talked, but you're a strange one, Kamiya," I told him.

"Like you're not?" he answered.

Oddly enough, we were able to joke around without being sarcastic or mean. Maybe we felt at ease around each other because we shared the same interests. While chatting in the classroom before going to his house, I'd discovered that he read the same literary magazine as me. That wasn't all. He was a fan of Keiko Nishikawa, who wasn't very well known back then.

He wasn't just good at keeping house. Everything he cooked was delicious.

"Please accept this humble brew."

"We're not having green tea, are we?"

He made us a pot of tea that day that was out of this world. It was something called Lady Grey that he'd gotten at the supermarket, and I was addicted ever since.

We sat around drinking tea and talking about all kinds of stuff. Around evening, he walked us to the station near his house. He brought along a reusable bag, saying he was going to pick up some groceries on the way back home. There was a mysterious dignity to him, like he was some veteran homemaker, and the reusable bag suited him oddly well. Maori and I couldn't help laughing at him for it. Maori took a picture, too.

Here was a guy who excelled at all things domestic and who looked perfect with an eco bag in hand. None of it was an act; on the contrary, it was part of who he was.

The next day after school, I invited the two of them to the condo where my mom and I lived. My dad didn't live with us, as my parents separated when I was in junior high school. While I took a cue from Tooru and made a pot of black tea in the kitchen, he and Maori talked in the living room. They were sitting close together, speaking too low for me to hear.

At the time, I was slightly jealous that Tooru had stolen my best friend. As that sentiment suggests, I saw him as her boyfriend, no more, no less. I held no romantic feelings for him. He was an oddball, somewhat cold like me, good at cooking and housework, and an avid reader of literature.

It was much later on that I developed romantic feelings toward him and when I began to feel a very slight amount of something like envy toward Maori.

Also…that I kissed Tooru.

6

I wanted to ask Wataya out on a date. We'd been together for almost two weeks. During that time, we'd exchanged some texts, chatted as usual, and talked a couple of times at the library after class.

Maybe I should have been satisfied with that. Maybe I shouldn't have hoped for more. But I wanted to try going out somewhere fun together. I wanted to talk about what we saw or felt while we were out. I wanted to see all kinds of places with her. Perhaps that feeling was what people referred to when they said they wanted to date. That they wanted to experience all kinds of things with a partner.

"So, would you like to go on a date?" I finally asked one day after searching for her on campus. She was sitting on a half-hidden bench near the administrative building.

"A date?"

She was probably confused because I hadn't bothered to say hello.

"Um, yes."

"With who?"

"With you."

"Me and who?"

"Me."

"Will do what?"

"Go on a date."

"With who?"

"With you."

"Me and who?"

"Me."

We went through that same conversation about three more times. At some point, I realized she was teasing me, but she was the one who gave up and stopped first.

"You're an honest fool. That's not a bad thing, though," she said, smiling. I smiled, too, embarrassed.

"Anyway, are you free next Saturday or Sunday?" I asked. An apologetic expression then came to her face.

"Sorry. There's something I always have to do on the weekends. I…don't think that will work."

My stomach roiled nervously. What was this thing she did on weekends? Was it related to the reason she wanted nothing more than a pretend relationship with me?

"Oh…okay. Do you mind if I ask what you have to do?"

"I have a high school friend who I get together with. She's attending a test prep school right now, and I help her with her studies on the weekends. It doesn't happen every week, though, so I like to keep my schedule free for her if I can."

A high school friend. I felt reassured by that. I'd heard something along those lines from our mutual friend. He'd said Wataya was still very close with that girl, and they often hung out. I wondered what she was like. Wataya had mentioned a test prep school, but I was genuinely curious to know more. I couldn't help asking.

"What kind of person is she?"

"What kind of person? Well, she's extremely cute. She has long hair, and she's very feminine. But she's not conceited. She's never two-faced, and she's got a good personality... Unlike me, she's the type that everyone likes."

She looked a little down. I might have been wrong, but that was how it seemed to me.

"You're pretty attractive yourself," I said immediately, maybe because I didn't like to see her looking dejected. "Everyone thinks you're remarkable, and I think they'd like to talk to you more if they could. But since you're so beautiful... I think everyone has a bit of a crush on you. Um, anyway..."

I realized I'd just said something fairly embarrassing. Wataya looked surprised, but a moment later, her expression softened.

"You don't have to worry about my feelings," she said.

"I'm telling you the truth."

"People see the world through a filter. Your filter is pure, I think. Although it might have a few too many blind spots."

They do say that love is blind, but I don't think that means my vision was clouded.

It was true that the other university students saw her as someone special. Because of her looks, but also because of her personality. Especially people in her year. On the surface, she seemed to do whatever she wanted, but the truth was, she constantly thought about others. I think she was unusually sensitive. She understood the subtleties of other people's feelings, and when she was with them, she tried to keep them in high spirits by laughing and smiling even if she had to force herself.

Several days before, a classmate had come up to her when the two of us were talking. She seemed happy while she chatted with them, and she made them laugh. After they left, I commented that she could get along with anyone. She grinned self-deprecatingly.

"I'm afraid of people, so I get along with them on a superficial level to make sure I'm not disliked," she said.

Just then, Wataya raised her eyebrows like she'd revealed something she shouldn't have. She tried to gloss over it by saying, "Just kidding!" I felt closer to her, having heard her true thoughts and seen her human-like weakness. My feelings for her were growing. But if I admitted that to her, she might break things off by saying I'd broken the rule she set.

After thinking this over, I said, "As your boyfriend, I see your best side. It doesn't have anything to do with a filter."

If I couldn't say I was falling for her, I could at least express my admiration for her.

"I always want to know more about you. That's why I want to take you on a date… Although of course it's fine if you need to prioritize your plans with your friend."

She gave me another startled look. After a moment, it turned into a wry smile.

"I swear, Naruse…"

She looked up at the sky like she was trying to make up her mind. Then she gave me a smile of resignation and stood up from the bench.

"The weekend won't work, but tonight does."

"What? You mean…"

"Let's go on a date. There just happens to be a movie I want to see."

Whatever it is you're wishing for, if you don't let yourself wish for it, it won't come true. That's obvious, and I know it's true.

Lucky for me, Wataya and I were going on a date that night. After our classes ended, we met in the library and walked to the subway. Maybe because I was so nervous, the ride was over before I knew it. There was a fancy high-rise outside the terminal station downtown, with a movie theater on one of the top floors. On the lower levels is an atrium with marble floors and lots of fancy shops.

"I feel like I'm on a date," I mumbled as I looked out from the elevator going up to the theater.

"You are on a date," Wataya said.

We'd already decided on the film. We were going to watch the film adaptation of the novel by Keiko Nishikawa that we'd talked about. Although it was a weekday evening, the theater was packed. I'd never been on such a date-like date, even when I had a girlfriend.

"Are you sure you don't mind paying?" I asked Wataya as we waited for the movie to start. We were sitting so close, our shoulders were touching.

"I'm the one who suggested it, so don't worry about it. Anyway, I have a job."

"Where do you work?"

"…My mom designs book covers, and I help her with the secretarial stuff. I've been doing it since high school, so I've got a decent amount saved up. For a student, I mean."

So her mom was a designer? That was the first time she had ever mentioned her family. Still…

"Next time, I'll treat you," I said.

She stared at me. Then she snorted and said, "Okay, we'll do that."

The previews started. I went over the plot of the novel in my mind while I waited for the main feature, and then I suddenly remembered the afterword. The author had mentioned going through some tough times before writing the book, but she didn't elaborate on what they were. I was curious and looked it up, but as far as I could tell, she hadn't revealed more details in any of her interviews. There were rumors of a family tragedy, but I didn't know if they were true.

The film began. It was a beautiful, sad story. Perhaps a reflection of the author's emotions at the time. It depicted the sorrow and pain of parting and the way that everyday life swallows up those feelings with its forceful and fleeting nature.

About halfway through the film, I noticed something. When I glanced at Wataya, her eyes were glittering, reflecting the light from the screen. Tears had welled up in her eyes, and the light shimmered on their surface like a living creature.

She was crying.

I was surprised, but not wanting to interfere with her experience of the film, I looked back at the screen. I thought about handing her my handkerchief, but I knew that as it was unironed, it would leave a bad impression. I resolved to always iron my handkerchiefs from then on.

Just…maybe this was obvious, but I realized that even Wataya cried sometimes. I was deeply moved. I would never have learned that on campus.

The movie had yet to reach its climax. I wondered what had moved her to tears. What did she feel sad about?

By the time the film was over, the sky outside was dark. At Wataya's suggestion, we went to a stylish café in the basement. I was happy just being able to spend more time with her. We sat down across from each other at a table and talked about what we'd watched over dinner. She seemed to like both the novel and the film, and she spoke enthusiastically about the directing and plot developments.

You cried, didn't you?

I wanted to say that to her. I wanted to ask what scene had moved her or made her sad. But I worried it would be rude. She might not have wanted to be seen crying. People cry for many reasons, and they are all quite personal. Just as I was thinking about this, she said, "The photos in the advertisements for the movie were beautiful, weren't they? The emphasis was more on the scenery than the people, I think."

"You're right. Like the depth of field was intentionally…"

I broke off, realizing I was talking like I was some expert on photography. She looked at me with a mixture of interest and surprise.

"Do you like photography?" she asked.

"No, I was just parroting something I heard to sound cool. I don't like taking pictures or having my picture taken."

Partly because I got distracted by that, I never did ask why she cried. Instead, I put on a smile and said, "Anyway, don't forget my promise. I'm paying next time we go out."

"Promise? We haven't even talked about where we're going or what we're doing."

"Okay, the zoo… No, the amusement park… No, how about the aquarium?"

"That was a lot of changes."

"The zoo smells like animals, and the amusement park is far away. I figured the aquarium is somewhere we can go on a weekday."

There was an aquarium relatively close by. A friend from university had told me they offered something called "Night at the Aquarium," where they kept it open until late. It was supposedly quite atmospheric and had become a popular date spot.

"The aquarium?"

"Do you dislike it?"

"It's not exactly that."

There was something I wanted to try, although I was shy about it. I'd considered various options, but the aquarium seemed to be the perfect place. If she wasn't opposed to it, I wanted to hold hands with her. Like a couple, if possible.

"Would you go with me? Playing pretend is fine," I said. I didn't want to be overly forward, and my voice slowly grew quiet. Maybe because she was worried about my feelings, Wataya gave that same resigned smile.

"…Okay. We'll do that next."

"Really, can we?"

"Sure. We are going out, after all."

I was happy to have arranged our next date. She smiled as she watched my excited reaction. We kept talking for a while, about movies we'd streamed, about novels we wanted to read, and about our mutual friend. As they say, time flies when you're having fun, and when I checked the clock, it was already nine. We left the café, and I walked her to the ticket gate.

"Well, good night."

"Take care on your way home."

I watched her walk into the station and stayed there until I couldn't see her any longer. It was a little thing, but it made me happy in a restless, bittersweet way. I walked over to my subway station, and as I waited on the platform, I sent her a message.

Thank you for today. I had a good time. I'm looking forward to the aquarium.

I noticed that she read it right away. I wondered if she'd had fun today. Would she say that she'd enjoyed the date and that she was also looking forward to next time?

A few minutes passed, and my train came. I had yet to receive a response. I got off at the station near the university and went upstairs to my apartment. I checked my phone. But for some reason, she never responded.

7

On their first date, Tooru and Maori went to a park known for its cherry blossoms. It was the second Saturday after they started going out, in early summer. Maori asked me for advice, but I didn't go with them. After that date, something changed.

Tooru learned about Maori's amnesia. And he had asked her not to write it down in her diary that he knew. He said he'd requested this because he didn't want Maori to be weighed down by that knowledge in the future.

At the time, I didn't know that. I was fenced in by all the things I didn't know. But when I think back on it, it makes sense. Starting the week after their date, Tooru's attitude toward Maori clearly changed.

I'd pegged him as somewhat cold, like I was.

But there he was, fixing a bike abandoned at the school bike-parking area so Maori could ride it.

To make her happy, he started to fulfill each and every one of her wishes. He pedaled as fast as he could down an abandoned country road while she sat on the cargo rack.

He was supposed to be a guy who never did anything crazy or reckless. He read novels, kept the house clean, brewed pots of tea, and kept quiet. He planned to be a bureaucrat when he graduated. That was the kind of practical life he lived.

But to make Maori happy, to fill her diaries with happy memories, he did outrageous things. He lived for her.

She smiled when she was with him. And not just her; he smiled, too. They began to walk a path toward love.

Their second real date was at the aquarium on the weekend. I tagged along for that one. I had noticed the change in Tooru and suspected he knew her secret. But by a strange coincidence, I learned his secret on that day, too.

We planned to meet by the clock tower outside the terminal station downtown. There was a big bookstore in a building attached to the station, and I stopped there before we were supposed to meet up. A sign read *Book launch and signing with Keiko Nishikawa, Akutagawa Prize–nominated author.* To my surprise, the author, who had been nominated for the prestigious prize for the first time, was going to be at the store.

I left the shop and walked to the clock tower. A few minutes later, Tooru showed up, looking slightly unsettled. Maori hadn't arrived yet. Since I knew he liked Nishikawa's books, I told him about the signing.

"Keiko Nishikawa is my sister," he said. It was the first I'd heard about his sister, who was six years older than him.

After his mother died, she'd taken care of him. She handled all the housework, as their father had become detached from reality from the shock of his wife's death. But Tooru's sister had a gift for writing. So much so that she was named a finalist for a famous literary prize while still in her teens. For the sake of Tooru and their father, however, she abandoned her dream of becoming a novelist.

But Tooru encouraged her to continue writing. He told his sister that if she taught him how to cook and run the household by the time he started high school, he would take over everything, including looking after their father. He set her free. Because of that, she was able to move out and live her own life, eventually winning the Akutagawa nomination.

"Well, these things happen," I told him. "You go see her; don't worry about us."

He said he'd stopped by the bookstore before they were to meet up, not knowing about the event, and had been reunited with his sister. Since they couldn't talk much during the signing, he'd promised to meet her after she was done.

"Don't worry. I'll cover for you with Maori. And thanks for the bento! Do you mind if I tell her your sister is Keiko Nishikawa?"

"Of course not. She's not the type to gossip. Besides, she's my girlfriend."

"Your girlfriend... Yeah. At first, I thought you two were dating as a joke or something. You've been really stepping up lately. I can tell you're trying to make her happy. Although, to me, you seem to be trying a little too hard."

Tooru had made a bento for all three of us to eat at the aquarium. After I took it from him, I tried to probe him. I thought he might have known about Maori's amnesia. We stared at each other in the middle of the crowd.

"Don't tell Hino this," he said before continuing in a serious tone. "I'm in love with her. Maybe that seems obvious, but I truly do love her. If there's something I can do to help her, I want to do it. That sounds arrogant. But I want to make her happy if I can."

The look in his eyes was different from when we'd first met. They were filled with his earnest feelings toward Maori. I felt that keenly.

"Why can't I tell her?" I asked.

"Because I'm embarrassed about it, obviously."

"You don't seem like the type to be embarrassed, Kamiya... You know about Maori, don't you?"

I looked him straight in the eye, trying to understand his true intentions. He stared back at me, his eyes still and unwavering.

"Yes, I know."

"How do you know? She didn't tell you, did she?"

"Yes, she told me. But I asked her not to write it down in her binder or her journal. Today's Hino...doesn't know that I know about her memory loss."

I was shocked. He smiled faintly.

"You better not tell her I know," he said, and walked off toward the bookstore. Maori showed up a short while later.

I told her about his sister, then headed for the aquarium. We walked around inside while we waited for him.

By that time, my immature fear that Tooru would steal her from me was gone. I easily separated my inner circle from everyone else. Before that day, Tooru was on the outside. We hung out, but my wariness toward him didn't fade. That changed the day we went to the aquarium.

The fact that he knew about her amnesia and was trying to make her happy changed the way I viewed him. Without fully realizing it, I had let him into my inner circle.

Gradually, I started enjoying the time the three of us spent together. On another weekend, we went to an amusement park together. During summer break, the three of us watched the live broadcast of the Akutagawa Prize announcements. We celebrated together when Keiko Nishikawa won.

We were a threesome. There was a powerful, deeply satisfying joy in that. But I might have been the only one who felt that way. Day by day, Tooru and Maori were becoming more like a pair. Maybe it's a strange thing to say, but that's how it felt to me. My sense of us being a group weakened. Maori was happy as long as Tooru was there, and

Tooru was happy as long as Maori was there. But that was to be expected. They were a couple.

When they told me they were going to see the fireworks on the last day of summer vacation, I said they should go ahead without me. I'd bought a yukata, thinking the three of us might go to a festival together sometime. To be completely honest, I was looking forward to it a little. But I wasn't needed. I would only get in their way because they were bonded by love. I was only Friend A, the heroine's best friend. Just a girl inexperienced in love and feeling the first stirrings of romantic interest in Tooru—although the feeling was so faint at that point, I didn't even notice it.

I spent the night of the festival alone in my condo. From the window, I could see the fireworks in the neighboring district exploding like tiny sparks. Although it was silly, I had put on my yukata and gazed at the fireworks by myself.

I knew the two must be watching them from up close. They were probably holding hands, experiencing it together as a couple. As I thought about them, I sensed that summer was ending. I was seventeen.

8

Did I do something wrong? Or was I misinterpreting things? Pitifully enough, I was obsessed with the fact that Wataya hadn't responded to my text. Perhaps she'd thought of me as nothing more than a nuisance the whole time I was elated on our date. The possibility scared me a bit. Then again, I might be overthinking things. When we ran into each other on campus, we chatted as if nothing was wrong. But after that first date, Wataya would sometimes space out in the middle of our conversations. She seemed lost in thought. It had happened again today.

"Wataya, are you all right?"

"What, me? I'm fine. Sorry."

She arranged her face into a smile. That was an accurate way to put it.

"Are you getting enough sleep? You did fall asleep in the library the other day. You must be exhausted."

"Oh, I just stayed up late writing the night before and didn't sleep enough."

"Writing, like a paper?"

"No, something personal. Something that had a deadline. Anyway, I'm getting plenty of rest now, so don't worry about me. I just have some things on my mind."

I tensed up, worrying those things had to do with me. I wanted to ask her about it, but I didn't have the courage.

"If there's anything I can do to help, please don't hesitate to ask."

Instead, I said something completely different. She gazed at me silently. For some reason, she smiled sadly.

"It's fine. You really are like I thought you were. A nice..."

She didn't finish her sentence. I looked at her questioningly.

"Never mind," she said.

I decided not to think too much about the text, or anything else, because I sensed she wouldn't want me to. There was no point in worrying about it.

But maybe I should have given it more thought.

We finally made it to the aquarium a full two weeks after first talking about it. Like the time before, we met after class and took the subway to the nearest station. Night at the Aquarium started at five. Outside, the sky was dyed a lonely orange, but inside, we were greeted by a lit-up fantasy world. It had a mature ambience.

"Hey, this is pretty nice," Wataya remarked. We walked through the exhibits together. It was fancier than I'd expected, which made me nervous. We were surrounded by other couples. Some of them were holding each other's hands as they peered into the tanks.

I was hoping to hold Wataya's hand that night. I kept glancing at her pale, delicate fingers, but when it came to actually reaching out to grab it, I hesitated.

"Why so quiet?" she asked.

"Nothing… I'm just n-nervous."

I glanced reflexively at her hand again. I think she noticed, but she didn't say anything about it.

"We're here, so we might as well enjoy it. Come on."

She headed down a softly lit hallway like she knew her way around. When I asked if she'd been there before, she said, "Just once. In high school."

High school. Was it with her ex? Slightly pained by that thought, I watched the colorful fish swim around in their tanks. After a few minutes, she stopped in front of one. Its large inhabitant was not so much swimming as elegantly soaring through the water.

"It's a ray, isn't it?"

"Yup, a ray through and through."

"...Can you eat rays?"

"Naruse, that's a bold question to ask in an aquarium. The employees would be shocked if they overheard you."

I felt flustered. Maybe it was a bit of an indiscreet comment. She looked at me and giggled. I was glad, but her smile didn't last long. She turned back to the tank.

"She's still here, same as always," she said.

Wataya was doing it again. For a moment, she had vanished from the present. What was she despairing over? She had come here in high school. Had something changed between then and now?

She walked silently to the next tank. I watched her without saying a word.

Eventually, the sun set, and it came time for the outdoor dolphin night show. The crowd was bigger than I'd expected. The same tastefully tinted indirect lights were on outside, and the dolphins looked completely different than they did during the daytime.

The show started. Surrounded by couples, Wataya and I watched the dolphins leap and dive. The couple right in front of us joined hands. My own hand flinched. Would it be presumptuous of me to hold Wataya's? Would she be offended? Nervous as I was, I took the plunge and grabbed her hand.

I'd read somewhere that love is wanting to hold someone's hand so desperately, you feel like you're going to die. And that the greatest joy of love is that feeling.

Wataya looked at me. She smiled.

Or not. No sooner had I seen her grin than she took her hand away. She was staring back at the dolphins.

I was overcome with regret. I wanted to apologize, but I couldn't speak right away. I apologized after the show ended. She slowly smiled and shook her head.

"Let's get going," she said. We left the venue. I felt so bad about my insensitivity and presumptuousness that I remained silent. It was after seven thirty when we stepped outside the aquarium.

"Um, would you like to grab dinner together?" I asked, honestly thinking she would refuse. I'd messed up that badly. But she said yes. Very normally and naturally.

We used the map app on my phone to walk to a restaurant. There was an Italian place nearby with big windows and a spacious interior that I'd thought of taking her when I was planning our date. Luckily, a table was open. We sat down across from each other and ordered from the unfamiliar menu.

I'd relearned a lesson that day. I was pitifully green when it came to romance. I lacked experience and was way too tense. With Wataya in particular, I lost sight of who I was almost immediately. I felt bad about that, but I also realized that my tension around her was a sign of how much I liked her. Wataya, who was sitting there right across from me.

She noticed me staring at her.

"What?" she asked.

"Nothing… I'm just starstruck."

"What?"

"By this place, I mean. The…the street at night and everything," I said, chuckling awkwardly.

"What are you talking about?" she asked, amused.

After that, I was able to talk with her as usual. She teased me; I got flustered. She laughed. We ate our dinner. My heart was pounding the whole time. I felt perhaps this state of suspension between nervousness and happiness was the pleasure of being in love.

Even if we were only playing make-believe, I wanted to spend more time with her. Our actions might have been inauthentic, but they could be the beginning of something. If we imitated love enough, it might become real.

That was why—

"I'm sorry. I'd like to break things off."

I didn't fully register what she said. It came out of the blue. We'd just been joking around, then she said that with a half smile. My happily thumping heart abruptly took on a cold, stormy cadence.

What did she just say?

Maybe I'd misheard her. Maybe I was misinterpreting her words. "Break things off" could refer to anything. Branches. Bread. Maybe I was so nervous that I'd taken her statement out of context.

"Um, what did you…?"

"I think we should break it off. Stop being a couple."

But it was no mistake. She was ending our relationship.

The world grew abruptly heavy. All the noises of the restaurant that hadn't bothered me before came flooding into my ears. The sound of forks scraping against knives, of couples talking happily, of waiters calling to cooks.

Until that moment, I had only seen Wataya. Everything else was a blur. That insular world had just vanished.

"But why? Is it because of what I did today…?" I managed to ask. She shook her head.

"No, not at all. I've been thinking a lot lately."

"Thinking about what?"

"You genuinely have feelings for me, don't you?"

I felt like I was being presented with an impossible choice. If I said yes, I was going against the condition of our relationship. If I said no, I was obviously lying.

I mean, I was crazy about her. What should I do? How could I fix the situation? Could we be a couple again? I stared at the table without answering her question. But I knew I had to say something. If I didn't, the whole thing would end right there.

"Why did you agree to date me in the first place?"

Nevertheless, I asked that spineless question. As if I was accepting that the end of our relationship was inevitable.

"I'm sorry. I don't really know why I did," she said. I raised my head. She looked terribly sad.

"There's something I can't forget…though I know I need to forget it. Maybe I thought that having a pretend relationship would make it all go away. If we kept things on a surface level and just had fun."

Just having fun. That was what she wanted, and maybe I hadn't been able to give that to her. Either way…

"Then let's do that starting now. Just have fun. The only thing I need to do is be careful, right? Not get too close?"

I was desperate. I had a reason to be desperate. But my feelings didn't reach her.

"I want things to be over. It was doomed from the start. I knew it would end like this."

"But…"

"And I told you from the beginning, I don't like nice guys."

As someone with nothing to offer, I thought I should have been kind at least. But it seemed she didn't need it. To the contrary, it got in the way.

"Why don't you like nice guys?"

I was reeling, but I still asked her the same question I had before. She responded right away.

"Nice people are good people. That kind of person…dies young."

I didn't know if she was being honest or just trying to make me give up. All I knew was that no matter what, I wasn't going to be able to continue our current relationship. When I didn't say anything, she stood up.

"Thank you for everything. I'm sorry to have put you through this. But it was fun."

She reached for the bill. Before I could say anything, she said, "Let this be my way of thanking you. Bye."

She smiled, then left without giving me a chance to respond.

I was left alone. She paid the bill and walked out the door. I stayed in my seat, listening to the sound of something ending.

It was dark outside the window, and the glass reflected the bright interior of the restaurant. I saw myself in the reflection. Me, who knew nothing about Wataya's real self.

Soon, it was summer vacation, and then very quickly, it seemed, break was over. I didn't speak to Wataya once during that time.

An Unknown Girl
and Her Unknowable Friend

1

Morning at home: As usual. Did drawing assignments, etc.

Afternoon: Met Izumi at three for tea at a café.

Evening at home: As usual. Continued with my drawing assignments.

With Izumi: met at the café by the station at three for tea (see "Restaurants" section for details on the place and what we had).

Izumi, a freshman in university now, is on summer vacation. She said her break is fairly long, and she thinks she'll have time on her hands. Apparently, university students have their own worries. I joked that every day was summer vacation for me. She laughed and said, "You're living the elementary schoolkid's dream."

We talked about my current situation. How my amnesia was not likely to go away anytime soon. But drawing is fun, and when I showed her the pictures I drew in my class, she complimented them.

She asked me what I wanted to do. After thinking about it, we decided to go to karaoke together tomorrow. But if I don't feel like it, she said it's okay if I cancel last minute. She's always so kind.

I joked that I'd like to have a summer fling. She pretended she was a handsome guy and asked if I'd be her lover.

As usual, it was fun talking to her. We talked about boys. When I asked if a lot of guys at university were pursuing her, she said no way. She's probably lying.

My past selves were wondering about it, so I asked what type of guy she's into. She said, "I don't mind telling you, but don't write it in your journal." She thought for a minute, then said, "Someone who's bad at housework."

When I asked why, she said, "Because I think I'm too sloppy to get along with someone who isn't," and laughed.

I wrote it down in the "Izumi" section even though she said not to. I'll write it here, too, to be safe.

Izumi's type: guys who are bad at housework.

I stopped reading over my year-old journal entries and looked up. Thunderheads were building outside my window, and painfully bright sunlight was shining in.

This spring, I recovered from amnesia. This is my first summer since recovering. I ate ice cream last night before going to bed. Really delicious strawberry ice cream. I'm able to remember what happened yesterday like it's the most natural thing in the world. Now I can build up my very own life, Maori Hino's life. That wasn't true before this spring.

I recorded what happened between May of my second year of high school and graduation, plus the year or so after, on my computer. There are two main characters in my journals. Me and my best friend, Izumi. No new characters appear, but on the other hand, none disappear. I typed an entry every day. The one I was just reading was part of the section from after graduation. I was taking it easy, attending drawing class as a hobby.

There was a reason I wasn't going to a test prep school or university. I was in my second year of high school when I got into an accident during Golden Week, and for about three years after that, I had amnesia. It was a particular type called anterograde amnesia. Simply put, I lost the ability to store new memories after my accident. But thankfully, Izumi stayed by my side through everything. With her help, and support from the high school administration, I managed to stay in school and graduate. Now that I've recovered from my amnesia, I'm attending test prep school. I'm hoping to start university two years later than my old high school classmates.

As I reread my journal, my phone buzzed. It was Izumi.

"Hey, Maori! How's it going?" she asked.

I love Izumi. Hearing her voice is enough to make me grin. But I took a deep breath and forced my voice to sound solemn. I was lacking something important. Something essential. Why? Why was that?

"...Izumi, I have to tell you something. I just can't figure it out, and it's really bothering me."

"Maori?"

"It's summer vacation…and I don't have a boyfriend!" I joked. I'd worked hard on that joke, which combined my lifelong lack of a boyfriend with the fact that it was summer.

There was a silence on the other end of the line for a few seconds, and then Izumi burst out laughing.

"You caught me off guard with that one."

"I thought you might be getting bored of the one where I say I can't remember what I had for dinner three days ago. I hope you appreciate the effort I put into this."

I smiled to relieve the tension I'd intentionally built up.

This was our usual routine, one that could only work with Izumi. She called me in the morning, and I pretended I still had anterograde amnesia. Maybe it was a tiny bit tactless, but it allowed me to turn my past disability into a joke.

Unfortunately, my memories from when I'd had amnesia haven't returned. Sometimes I feel like I'm on the verge of remembering something, but the memories never rise fully to the surface. However, I didn't need to be sad about that. Everything important from that period should have been written down in the journal on my computer. Everything should be preserved there as data. More importantly, I have Izumi for a best friend.

"Sorry for being such a weird conversation partner, Izumi."

"No worries. Part of why I call you is because I want to hear your jokes."

"They're jokes, but they're also cries of sorrow."

"Hmm. Even though you don't want to date anyone?"

"Good point. I don't understand it myself. It's very strange."

Izumi and I were meeting that afternoon. Since I was on my brief break from test prep school, we were planning to have lunch and then do a little shopping for clothes and books and stuff to relax.

"By the way, Maori, what's our look for today?"

"Since you're wearing a tuxedo, I figured I'd wear my wedding dress."

"Be careful you don't step on its train and fall."

We've been like this since high school. Our conversations were basically just banter. After making sure we weren't wearing the same outfit as each other, we hung up.

I got my things together in time to meet her for lunch, said goodbye to my parents, and left the house. There was an interesting Italian restaurant near my test prep school that I'd been wanting to try, so I made a reservation and we arranged to see each other there. As I was walking toward the train station, I looked up at the sky. Thunderheads floated against an endless expanse of blue, and sunbeams poured down like pure light.

While I was staring up, I heard excited voices ahead of me. I looked toward them. A boy and a girl, highschoolers by the looks of it, were riding on a bike together. As they passed me, I heard them shout giddily, "Go! Go! We got this!"

How strange…

I felt like I'd ridden on a cargo rack like that myself once and said the same things. For just a moment, I felt like I glimpsed the back of a boy wearing a school uniform and pedaling a bike.

I tried to remember who it was, but I came up short. I must have been mixing up my memory of Izumi's back. There was an entry in my high school journal about riding on a bike with her. On the verge of recalling something, I started walking toward the station again.

I got to the restaurant on time. When I told the waiter my name, he said Izumi was already there. He pointed me toward her, and I walked over.

"Hey, you're not wearing your wedding dress!" she exclaimed when she saw me. We text each other every day, but we hadn't met in person for two weeks, partly because I'd been busy with school.

"I'm getting ready for my entrance exams. It would be bad luck if I tripped."

"Darn. I brought along my tux to change into."

"Looks like we'll have to postpone the wedding reception."

I sat down. The waiter brought me a menu, and I bravely ordered the lunch special. Though I was feeling daring, Izumi seemed nonchalant.

"What, now that you're a sophomore, Italian food is no big deal?"

"No! The only place I ever go to with university friends is the pub."

"You don't go to stylish places?"

"You're the only one I go on dates with to places like this."

She winked, and I couldn't help smiling. As we were chatting away, the appetizers arrived. We had a good time, taking pictures of our food and all that. Eventually, the conversation turned to my studies, the university I wanted to go to, and Izumi's school.

"You're still not dating anyone?" I asked. She raised her eyebrows and smiled wryly.

"Unlike you, I'm not that cute. I don't have any experience."

"That again? I don't have any experience, either. I've never dated anyone."

"…You always turn guys down when they ask you out."

"So do you! Remember our first year of high school when that guy in second year asked you out?"

"I do remember that! Ah, the good old days."

"They're still recent to me! My memory is crystal clear."

Izumi always puts herself down by calling herself cold, or by saying that other people can't tell what she's thinking. But I know she's the most warm-hearted person in the world. And the proof is that she tried to make every day of my life fun when I had amnesia. She helped me do the things I wanted to do and have a good time. My past selves were saved by that. I'm grateful to her from the bottom of my heart. But she seems uninterested in romance and never dates anyone. I'm sure guys at her university ask her out, but she never talks about it or anything else related to herself.

"So what's your type?" I couldn't help but inquire out of curiosity.

"I knew you were going to ask me that."

"I've only asked you about three times in my life!"

"…I guess that's true."

Actually, I was lying. I'd asked her three times since my amnesia went away this spring, but I know I asked her before that. I wrote about it in my journal after we graduated from high school. She apparently told me not to write her answers down, but my past selves seemed very interested and recorded it anyway.

- Hates nice people.
- Doesn't get along with people who are good at housework.
- No to anyone good at cooking.
- Doesn't like considerate people.

- Incompatible with people who value their family.
- Looking for someone who's not serious.

If I sum up the notes in my journal, that's her type. Maybe I lack imagination, but I feel like the only kind of person who would meet those criteria is a real loser. That, or a workaholic who ignores his family and friends.

But when I asked her that same question today, she gave me a different answer.

"I'd prefer someone who's not younger than me."

That was a surprise since she'd never mentioned age before.

"But…why?"

"Why? I don't know. Image, I guess."

"Image?"

"Yeah. Younger guys seem kind of…servile. And naive and honest. I don't think we'll be compatible. I mean, someone like that shouldn't be wasted on me…"

"Did something happen at university?"

"Nothing at all. How could it?"

She tried to brush it over with a smile, but I knew her too well for that. My guess was something did happen with a guy younger than her at school. Still, if she didn't want to bring it up, she must not want to talk about it.

"Anyway, what about you? Anyone at the test prep school?"

"Me? Zilch. As far as they know, I failed my university entrance exams twice already. I'm a little older than everyone, too."

"That's great coming from someone who just got asked out a few weeks ago."

We finished our lunch along those lines. Afterward, we went shopping in the neighborhood. Izumi has a tomboyish style, while I tend to like more feminine stuff. At the clothing stores, we chose outfits for each other to try on and took pictures to entertain ourselves. I bought a pair of pants that Izumi said looked good on me. We checked out some accessory shops, too. Time goes by so quickly when we're together. Before taking a tea break, we stopped at a bookstore. I wanted to look at some reference books, and Izumi said there was something she wanted to buy.

"Wow, they're still on display. She's so popular," Izumi remarked, looking at the stack of novels by Keiko Nishikawa, an author she likes. "The movie adaptation of this has gotten good reviews, and it's still playing. I bet they'll be selling these all summer."

She smiled, then glanced at one of the books. There was a photograph of the author on display. Maybe because she was so pretty, I felt strangely fascinated by her.

"What's wrong, Maori?" Izumi asked.

"Hmm? Oh, I doubt I have…but have I ever met this woman?"

"…I think you might have."

"No way."

"In a magazine or on TV."

She grinned, and I realized I'd fallen for one of her jokes. We both went to purchase our books, then headed for a café nearby. Drinks in hand, we chatted happily. I'd bought a reference book and Izumi had bought a few novels.

Suddenly, I remembered something.

"Izumi, didn't you say you were writing a novel? How's it going?"

She looked a bit surprised.

"You remembered that?"

"I remember things now. You told me after my amnesia went away."

"I know, but I'm still surprised you did."

She'd told me about it during Golden Week. She was hanging out at my house, and when I showed her one of the pictures I'd drawn for fun, she surprised me by saying, "I wanted to find some kind of creative hobby like you...so recently, I've started writing a novel."

In junior high, I was in the Art Club, and I used to draw every day. But in high school, I was too busy to join one, and I stopped drawing. However, I picked it up again because of my amnesia. I'd assumed that anterograde amnesia would prevent me from developing anything over time, but in fact, I was able to. It has to do with something called procedural memory, which is the name for things you remember with your body. It's the reason that even people who lose their memories are able to ride a bicycle.

According to my diary, I was overjoyed to have found out about procedural memory. I was deeply grateful to Izumi for discovering it, and I drew every day. My skills improved, which was immensely gratifying. Though I've recovered from my memory loss, I still draw sometimes just for fun. As a result, I keep accumulating sketchbooks. It was one of those sketchbooks that Izumi was looking at when she told me she was writing a novel.

"That's perfect, since you're so erudite," I told her.

"That's not true," she said modestly. "Keiko Nishikawa is a judge in a new contest that a magazine is sponsoring. They put out a call for photographs and paintings, too."

That was the only time she'd talked about her novel. I wanted to ask her more about it, but maybe because she felt self-conscious, she changed the subject. Still, it remained in my mind. In the most natural way possible, I asked her what her novel was about.

"It's nothing important," she said. "I'd hardly even call it a novel yet. It's just a way of collecting my thoughts and ideas."

"So…does that mean you're the main character?"

"No… The main character is a disgustingly kind person."

I asked if it was a man or a woman, and she said it was a man. If the main character was female, she thought it would end up being too realistic or annoying. I got the sense she didn't want to talk much more about it. But I was so curious that I decided to ask one last question.

"What happens to him at the end?"

She looked at me silently. When she answered, I glimpsed a quiet sadness rooted deep in her eyes.

"He dies suddenly."

Izumi and I have known each other since high school. That might not be very long in the grand scheme of things. And maybe it's presumptuous to call her my dearest friend. But I believe we'll be friends for life. There's no one else I get along with so well, have so much fun with, and respect and count on.

However, I realized then that in the three-year gap when I'd lost my memory, a part of her that I didn't know emerged. Sometimes she looks sad. I don't know if it has to do with her family or with school or with something else. Or I could be imagining it.

"Anyway, Maori, let's eat our cake. I got hungry walking around," she said, cheerfully interrupting my thoughts. I managed to smile back and nodded.

"Izumi?" I asked.

"What is it, Maori?"

"We'll always be best friends, won't we?"

"Of course! What made you ask that?"

"I was just wondering…if you might give your dear friend a bite of your cake."

"So that's your ulterior motive? Fine, but only if I can have a bite of yours."

We enjoyed the rest of our time at the café and left around evening. When I got home, I noticed I had a message from her. I couldn't help but grin when I read it. She thanked me for hanging out and sent a picture of us together at the café. We were both smiling happily.

2

Izumi brings me nothing but happiness. When she's with me, she always smiles like she's having fun, and she never reveals her worries or problems. But just because she doesn't show them to me doesn't mean they don't exist. There are as many stories as there are people in this world, each one with its own joys and conflicts. Everyone has things they keep to themselves.

I was made newly aware of that fact several days later, on the last day of my summer break when I met a freshman from Izumi's school.

Last night, I'd been talking to her on the phone, and we were having such a good time, we decided to hang out the next day in person. But then she remembered something. When I asked her about it, she said, "Sorry, I know it's summer break, but I have to go to campus tomorrow."

I'd always been curious about her university, and this seemed like a good opportunity to see it as long as I didn't get in her way. We agreed that I'd accompany her.

I took the subway from my house and walked to her campus.

"Sorry to make you come all the way here," she apologized.

"Not at all! I've been wanting to know more about your school, so this is perfect."

We met at the front gate, signed in with the guard, and went in. The campus was way bigger than our high school grounds, with fancy glass towers. I'd expected it to be empty since it was summer break, but there were a few people here and there.

Since it was lunchtime, Izumi invited me to eat with her at the "nice" dining hall. I couldn't believe how spacious it was, a far cry from the no-frills kind of place I'd imagined.

"This campus is much bigger than I thought it would be. It's interesting. I feel like I could live here."

"Please don't. I don't want you to turn into the seventh wonder of the university."

"Along with the female ghosts who wander the campus every night?"

"Yeah, the ones who float around saying 'Give me a shower! Give me shampoo!'"

Izumi said she had to turn something in to her adviser, so we agreed to meet up at the library later. After lunch, I wandered on my own, intent on walking around campus until she was done. But then I decided to head to the library before we were to meet, as the large structure had caught my eye earlier in the day, and it was open to the public.

It had been rebuilt a few years before, and the inside was quite modern. It had a good selection of magazines, and even some international fashion magazines.

As I was about to leave that section, someone came up behind me and said, "Um, excuse me." I turned around to see a guy standing there. He was fairly tall, and slender, and looked to be a kind person. I guessed he was younger than me. What could he want? I'd checked in at the front desk, but did the staff think I was suspicious? I stared at him questioningly.

"Are you a friend of Wataya's?"

"Wataya? …Oh, yes. Why?"

"Nothing. I'm a freshman here, and I saw you earlier at the dining hall. I live near campus, so I go there every day, even during summer break. And…"

He must have been nervous, because he was giving me all kinds of unnecessary information. So he was a classmate of Izumi's and a year below her. I'd never heard Izumi mention him. But I guess that was to be expected, as she hardly ever talks about herself.

"Are you a classmate of Izumi's?" I asked. He suddenly perked up.

"I am! Did she tell you about me?"

"…I'm sorry. I don't think she has."

"Oh."

His happy expression quickly turned glum. Maybe it was rude to say this, but the way his emotions played out on his face was very entertaining. We couldn't keep chatting where we were, so we decided to go somewhere else. He said there were several break rooms in the building. We went up to one on the third floor that he said wasn't used very often.

"Um…actually, Wataya and I were dating before summer vacation started," he said incredibly. Izumi had claimed she wasn't interested in having a relationship, but she'd been seeing this very person! I was left momentarily speechless.

"You…and Izumi?"

"Yes. Although it wasn't very serious."

For a moment, I thought he was joking, but why would he have gone out of his way to find me and then tell me a lie, or possibly a joke? More importantly, he didn't seem like the type to do that. Which meant the two of them really must have been seeing each other.

"I had no idea," I revealed.

"From her perspective, it might not have reached the level of dating. That's probably why she didn't mention it."

"…Maybe. She's never been one to talk much about herself."

At that point, I realized we hadn't introduced ourselves. He said his name was Naruse, that he and Izume were in the same department, and they'd first talked at a party. I told him I was a friend of hers from high school. Like I did at test prep school, I left out the part about my amnesia.

"High school friends?" he echoed pensively. "Then you must know who she dated in high school. It seems like she still can't forget about them."

I was so shocked, I was positive my eyeballs would pop out of my head.

Izumi had dated someone in high school?

This was bewildering. Was it true? At least up till Golden Week of our second year, I didn't think she'd dated anyone. She had always turned down everyone who asked her out. Then, after I developed amnesia, she spent every day with me. How could she have had time for a relationship? There wasn't any mention of it in my diary, either.

"I'm sorry, I don't know anything about that," I said.

"You don't?"

"Is it really true? I mean…I have no clue what you're talking about."

Now it was his turn to look surprised. As we were staring at each other in confusion, my phone buzzed. It was a message from Izumi.

Sorry I took so long. I'm about done, so I'll head to the library soon. Where are you?

I stared at Naruse.

Izumi had her own life, and she must have secrets and things she didn't want me to pry into. Maybe he was one of those things. Maybe what had happened in high school was, too…

I wanted to leave it alone, but it could be related to my past. I'd thought everything that happened when I had amnesia was written down in my computer, but perhaps there were things I hadn't included for various reasons.

"I'm sorry, Izumi's going to be here in a minute. You probably don't want her seeing us together, do you?"

I figured that was the case since he hadn't approached me when I was with her. He panicked slightly when he heard she was on her way.

"Uh, yes… I'm sorry, but I'd rather she didn't."

"Do you think we could meet some other time? I'd like to hear more about this possible relationship she had during high school."

He seemed surprised by my suggestion but said, "Of course," and nodded.

We exchanged messaging IDs. Since Izumi could show up any minute, I quickly said goodbye and left the break room.

Sorry I didn't answer sooner, I wasn't sure if it was okay to use my phone in the library, I texted.

No worries. It's always hard to figure out stuff like that in a new place.

I'm in the bathroom on the third floor. Should I go outside?

It's hot out, so why don't you wait by the magazines on the first floor? I'll be right there. And don't worry, you can use your phone as long as you don't take pictures.

I went back to the magazine area. A few minutes later, Izumi arrived.

"Sorry you had to wait," she said.

"Don't worry, I wasn't waiting. I barely had time to walk around campus!"

"Oh, good. Did you have a decent time?"

"...Yeah. Everything here is so surprising."

"Is it?" she said, and smiled. We decided to go to a café nearby. Like that morning, people turned to watch Izumi as she walked through campus.

"I think you'll like this place. The atmosphere is nice, and they have good cake."

Izumi had become even prettier than she was in high school, and more mature-looking. Perhaps because her mom was a designer, she had an eye for beauty and a good fashion sense.

I thought back to spring of this year, about six months ago. When she came to see me right after I'd recovered from my amnesia, her makeup was the same as in high school, and she was wearing familiar clothes. In hindsight, she must have done that so as not to surprise me, since things were still frozen in our second year of high school for me.

She was trying to shield me from the drastic shift in time that had occurred.

As my own sense of time advanced, so did her appearance. She started wearing the kind of clothes and makeup she had on today. That's the sort of sweet person she is. She has always supported me and considered my feelings. But...there were things about her I didn't know.

You must know who she dated in high school. It seems like she still can't forget about them.

What was he talking about? Had he misinterpreted something she said, or was it true?

Izumi noticed that I was staring at her.

"What's wrong, Maori? Why are you looking at me like that?"

"Huh? Oh, nothing. I was just thinking how cool you are."

"Where did that come from? Are you by chance...after my cake again?"

"Darn, you caught me," I joked.

"You're easy to catch." She grinned.

It was the same smile as always: free of worry, free of even the slightest hint of sadness.

3

I talked to Naruse again three days later, after test prep school. He offered to come to where I was, so we met at a family restaurant near my school.

"Thank you for making time for me, Hino," he said. "I know you must be busy. Are you sure it's okay for the two of us to meet like this? I forgot to ask if you had a boyfriend, in case he minds."

"There's no need to worry about that. I've never had a boyfriend, so it's all good. Also, you don't have to call me by my last name."

"Should I call you Maori, then?"

"Yes, that's fine."

We sat down facing each other, and after the initial formalities, we dived straight into the reason we were there.

"So, about that boyfriend Izumi had in high school…I really have no clue what you're talking about. How did you learn about him?"

"Well…," he began timidly. He told me about his initial gaffe, when he told Izumi he bet she'd never had a passionate love affair, and her answer, and their fake relationship. All of this surprised me, but one thing in particular caught my attention.

"She told me the same thing when I asked her out as when she cut things off. She doesn't like nice guys."

It was the same thing I'd written down in my journal.

- Hates nice people.
- Doesn't get along with people who are good at housework.
- No to anyone good at cooking.
- Doesn't like considerate people.
- Incompatible with people who value their family.
- Looking for someone who's not serious.

There was also what she'd said the other day: *I'd prefer someone who's not younger than me.* I wondered if that had something to do with Naruse. I ultimately decided not to mention it to him and instead talked about the conditions she'd mentioned before. Naruse pondered this for a few moments before summing it up.

"So it's possible that the guy she dated in high school wasn't nice, was bad at housework and cooking, was inconsiderate, didn't value his family, and wasn't serious."

I'd had the same thought. The problem was, who in the world would fall for someone like that?

"If Izumi did have a boyfriend in high school... And if she still can't forget him...," I mused.

"Yes?"

"Then what if he was the opposite of everything she said? What if she still loves that person, and she can't move on from him? Maybe she's purposely trying to date someone who's completely different."

Naruse seemed to find this revelatory.

"That...could be what's going on. There are times when she looks incredibly sad, like she's suffering. Maybe she's remembering her old boyfriend."

That made me think. He was right that Izumi did look really sad sometimes. Was it because she was remembering her old love? But Naruse wasn't likely to know anything more about it. My only options were to scour my journals for some kind of clue or ask Izumi directly. Another possibility was to ask some of our high school classmates, but I'd never told them about my amnesia. Even though I'd recovered, I still felt slightly wary of seeing them again

"I'm sorry to pull you into this," Naruse said, perhaps guessing what I was thinking. "If I hadn't approached you in the library, you would never have had to worry about this. It was thoughtless of me."

I was quick to reassure him.

"Please don't worry about that. I want to know more about her myself. I was thinking about something else right now."

"Really? I know I might not be much help, but if there's anything I can do, please let me know. I'll do everything I can to help you."

Having delivered this admirable speech, the young Naruse gave me a bright smile. It told me he was a sincere and warm-hearted person.

"You're a nice guy, aren't you."

"Not at all. I'm only as nice as the next guy, and it doesn't do anyone much good."

For some reason, kind people always say things like that. Like they always see their own kindness as somehow inadequate or powerless, even though it's the most noble quality imaginable. Like they genuinely feel they have nothing to offer.

But I couldn't remember what situation from the past was giving me this sense of déjà vu. Maybe it was something that had happened when I had amnesia. No matter how much I shored up my own past with digital data, perhaps it was impossible to fully share in the feelings and thoughts of my past self. My mood grew darker as I ruminated on this.

"Thank you, Naruse. I'll get in touch if I find out anything. Anyhow, since we're here…"

So that he didn't have to worry about me anymore, I made sure we had a pleasant chat. I took the opportunity to ask him about Izumi's university persona. He mirrored my cheerfulness. According to him, Izumi engaged casually with her classmates just like she had in high school but basically kept to herself. He said everyone thought she was cool because of it. That sounded like her, I thought fondly.

"Sometimes, she hangs out on campus in places where no one else goes. I used to go looking for her just to be able to say hello."

"That does sound like Izumi. And what does she do all by herself?"

"Reads books, thinks, and reads something that looks like a diary."

"A diary? I didn't realize she kept one."

This was another side of her I was unaware of. It made me a little sad to realize how much I didn't know about my best friend.

"...I know she was writing a novel, though," I said, accidentally letting something slip.

"Really, a novel?" he asked.

"Oh, sorry. I didn't mean to tell you that. It's just..."

He smiled, seeming to sense my hesitation.

"It's okay, I won't tell anyone, and I won't ask about it."

"Thanks, it's a relief to know that."

As we smiled awkwardly at each other, Naruse seemed to realize something.

"Ahh," he said.

"What?"

"Nothing. Just that Wataya said she had stayed up late writing once, and I wondered about it. I thought maybe she was working on something like a novel. Ah, I miss those days. That was before summer break."

He smiled sadly. He'd said it was only a pretend relationship, but I could tell he genuinely liked her.

"Cheer up, Naruse."

"I'm sorry to be so morose. Don't worry about me, I'm fine."

As if to demonstrate that he was okay, he told me about the dates they'd gone on. He said they'd seen the movie based on Keiko Nishikawa's book.

"Izumi really loves that author," I said.

"Seems like it. As far as I could tell from Nishikawa's photo, Wataya even looks kind of like her. The cool type or something."

"I know what you mean. By the way, Nishikawa is one of the judges for a new literary prize. Izumi told me about it."

"A prize? That's interesting… Wait a second. Those things have submission deadlines, right? Then maybe…"

He started to say something, then broke off with a smile and said, "Never mind." I sensed his calm, gentle character in that smile.

4

August was almost over. Taking time off was well and good, but I couldn't let myself get out of the groove of studying. I had to learn everything I'd missed during my second and third years of high school in one year. So I kept at it morning, noon, and night. I still made time to text with Izumi, though. Occasionally, I messaged Naruse, too. He'd started a part-time job a few days after we talked at the diner and seemed busy with that. I reread my journals during my study breaks, but I couldn't find any clues as to whether Izumi had a boyfriend in high school.

One day when I was chatting with my mom, I brought up Izumi and Naruse. My parents know Izumi well and trust her. They are deeply grateful for what she did for me when I had amnesia. At first, my mom seemed pleased to hear that Izumi was dating a younger guy at university. But that changed when I mentioned the boyfriend from high school.

"Izumi never mentioned anything to me directly, but it seems likely she was interested in someone in high school," I said. "A kind person who was good at housework… Someone who was family-oriented, I guess? Does that ring any bells, Mom?"

My mother froze. She stared at me wordlessly, then looked away.

"Mom?"

"Hmm? Oh, let's see… I don't know."

She smiled reservedly. Was I imagining things, or did she look slightly sad? When I asked her what was wrong, she just shook her head.

"Nothing. I was just thinking about how old I'm getting," she said, then added as if awestruck, "Izumi, too…"

I wanted to ask Izumi about it directly. But that would put Naruse in an awkward position. I imagined the conversation between us.

Hey, Izumi, did you like anyone in high school or date anyone?

What, why?

I was just wondering. You were so busy looking after me all the time.

She was sharp enough to know that if I said something like that out of the blue, I would have learned it from Naruse. But maybe if I broached the topic very carefully…for example…

One day in September when I had relatively little studying to do, I met up with Izumi in the afternoon to check out a new café.

It was popular among high school students. I'd seen groups of them in their uniforms chatting happily inside several times on my way home from test prep school. There were lots of photos of the place on social media, too. On this day, it was full of high school girls having animated conversations about fall semester tests and school and sports festivals. Watching them from the corner of my eye, I said out loud what I felt at that moment.

"Sometimes…I wish I could go back and have a normal high school experience."

Izumi, who was joking around a moment ago, looked surprised. I was slightly shaken myself. My words had come out sounding more serious and emotional than I had intended. I smiled to gloss over the solemn mood and continued in a lighthearted tone.

"I mean, thanks to you, I enjoyed every day. If I never had amnesia, I would remember all of it. But more than anything, I just feel bad for what you had to do. Ha-ha!"

"Maori…"

"Oh, don't take me too seriously. It's just that you always had to accommodate my needs. I worry that you didn't get to do the things you wanted to do. You never mentioned that you liked anyone back then, but did you? If it hadn't been for me, maybe you and that person…"

I was trying to learn more about her, but I really did feel like I'd stolen her time and opportunities, and I felt horrible about it. Simultaneously, I felt renewed gratitude toward her.

"Maori, why are you asking me this all of a sudden?"

For a second, she looked serious, but then, maybe to match my mood, she brightened up.

"No reason, really, but you know I still reread my high school diaries on my computer. Everything in there is about me, and it made me wonder what was going on with you."

I smiled, trying to lighten the mood. Her eyebrows were furrowed, but she still smiled back. With her mouth, at least. With that smile on her face, she sank into thought. She stared at the table. My heart was beating quietly but strongly. *There might be things that Izumi has never told me. Maybe I'll finally learn what they were today.* That was what I thought.

"No, there wasn't anyone. I didn't have any high school crushes."

That's why I was so taken aback when she looked up at me with a smile and said that. She was gazing at me earnestly. I'd thought that by asking her about it, I would learn of her true feelings. I'd thought I would hear high school stories I didn't know. But her gaze was completely calm and clear. It held no sense of deception or falsehood.

But perhaps it was too calm. Too clear, like an empty blue sky.

"Thanks for always being so considerate," she said. "In high school, you used to say the same thing, that you felt bad I had to accommodate you."

She glanced away, then grinned softly, tenderly. Then, she looked back at me and continued.

"But you know what? I had a lot of unique experiences thanks to you."

She must have been talking about affectionately supporting a friend with memory loss—me. She would never mention this, but I know I must have been a real pain in the butt when I had amnesia. Yet Izumi had stuck by me all the same. And she was still making time for me.

She paused slightly, then went on.

"My life was boring until I met you. I felt like I knew all about life, and I never did anything stupid or crazy. But after I met you in high school… Maybe it's bad to put it this way, but after things got a little hard for you, I felt like I learned something important about myself."

She was looking directly at me, smiling calmly.

"Thank you, Maori. Thank you for being my friend."

I…didn't know that. I didn't know she could smile like that. Like she held something dear and treasured and respected it from the bottom of her heart.

There was a light inside her. A light people couldn't see. A warm, kind glow that maybe she herself didn't even realize had emerged, like a wellspring. It hadn't been there when I'd known her in high school. I wondered where she had gotten it from. Where had she found it? When had she changed?

As I sat there, quietly struck by this realization, she said thoughtfully, "I'm sorry, was that a bit too heavy?"

"What? Not at all. Just…thank *you*, Izumi."

"Anyway, I enjoyed high school in my own way. But I'm sorry to say there was never anyone I liked or dated," she joked.

That was the end of our conversation about high school. She never liked anyone or dated anyone then. That was what she decided. Or maybe it was the truth.

After we separated for the night, I sent a message to Naruse. I told him she'd said that she didn't like or date anyone in high school.

Later, after I got back home, I got a reply. *Thank you for letting me know. I realize you're busy with studying. I'm sorry I pulled you into this!*

I looked at it for a long time. There are so many kind people in the world. The world is overflowing with human emotions. As I was thinking about Izumi, my thoughts suddenly shifted to myself.

…What about me?

Did I like anyone in high school?

Maybe I didn't have the capacity for it, since I had anterograde amnesia. There wasn't any mention of a crush in my journal. But why hadn't I developed feelings for anyone since recovering? No matter how kind or handsome or trustworthy a person was, I felt nothing for them.

It was like my heart was already devoted to someone else.

Later that fall, I found a drawing in my room of a guy I didn't know. I was sure from the style that I had drawn it several years earlier. For some reason, it was tucked into the gap between my bookshelf and the wall, like I'd hidden it as if it was a treasure that I didn't want anyone to take away. It was in the place where I used to keep important things when I was little.

When I saw that unfamiliar face, my heart started pounding.

I was confused by how hard it was beating. I felt like it was trying to tell me something. I wasn't sure if I recognized him or not, and I didn't think I knew him…but strangely enough, I also felt like I knew him very well.

It wasn't until later that I learned who he was. That I learned who Tooru Kamiya was. How he was the boy I'd met when I had amnesia, the boy who I fell in love with…

At the Center of the Light

1

Before I knew it, summer was over, and fall had begun. My second year of university was almost half over. The autumn winds were cold, and maybe their piercing chill made me sentimental. I sat down alone on a bench on campus and thought back on everything that had happened this year.

In spring, I met Naruse and we started dating.

Before summer vacation, we broke up.

Maori and I still spent time together, smiling and laughing.

…But that wasn't all. I had lied again. When Maori asked me if I liked anyone in high school, I told her I didn't. But she'd simply forgotten. In high school, she'd noticed my feelings.

Izumi, do you by chance have a crush on Tooru?

The first time she asked me that was just before the end of our second year of high school, over spring break. That day, the two of them had insisted that I come with them to picnic under the cherry blossoms at the park where they'd gone on their first date.

And since the end of summer vacation, the pair had changed more notably. Maori, in particular. She'd never met Tooru prior to developing amnesia. So even though they were dating, he was almost a total stranger to her when she woke up every morning. Nevertheless, it seemed to me that now when she saw him, she got used to their relationship more quickly than she had before. She seemed to trust him completely.

The day of the picnic, when she and I were on our way home after saying goodbye to Tooru, out of the blue, she inquired timidly if I liked him.

"What made you think that?" I asked. "Also, me and Tooru?"

"I'm sorry to ask this so suddenly. Maybe I'm imagining it. I just… kind of feel like you might."

I smiled wryly, waving dismissively to emphasize my point.

"No way. I care way too much about handsome faces to like him. Kamiya is a good guy…but I only like him in the sense that we have similar interests. He's just a friend to me."

Maori seemed reassured by my nonchalant answer.

"Really? That's good to hear."

"Seriously, though, why'd you ask?"

"No reason. It's just that when I met him today, I could tell what a good person he was, and you're very important to me, too. So if you liked him…I would be worried I was getting in the way."

"Oh, don't worry about that. You two are already dating, so if anyone is getting in the way, it's me."

I tried to sound as natural as possible. But maybe because I knew she was paying close attention, I felt overly sensitive to the nuance of my own words.

If anyone is getting in the way, it's me.

If I was honest with myself, I was already starting to fall for him.

Because we have similar interests?

Not just that.

Because he's so good to my best friend, Maori?

That was part of it. But that wasn't the main reason.

Because I realized how kind he is?

...Normally, people aren't able to step outside of themselves. It's impossible for them to care more about someone else than about themselves. They constantly weigh their options and choose what's advantageous for them.

Or so I thought. Tooru showed me a side that I didn't know existed. He cared about Maori more than he cared about himself, and he didn't expect anything in return.

No matter how much he loved her and valued her, she forgot it all the next day. Even so, he did everything he could to make her daily life fun. He never complained, even though he must have gone through tough things himself. He was always smiling around her.

"Kamiya, how do you do it?" I asked him once when the two of us were alone, not long before we had our picnic under the cherry blossoms. The sky was a beautiful dusky pink behind him as he turned toward me.

"Because I love her," he answered placidly, completely unruffled.

It hurt me. I never knew that watching someone smile could be so painful.

Why does it hurt so much?

I tried not to think about it. Instead, I asked in a self-mocking tone, "Just because you love someone, does that mean you'll do anything for them? Personally, I don't get that."

"I don't do anything. I do what I can," he clarified.

"Is that true? You seem to be pushing yourself kind of hard for someone who's just doing what they can."

"I don't do what's impossible, and I couldn't even if I tried. But if there's something I can do with a little extra effort or something I want to do, then I feel happy to do it."

I stared at him silently. I couldn't grasp what he meant, but I wanted to.

At the same time, I was starting to realize something. The pain I'd felt earlier and my desire to understand him both suggested that I...

"My life before I met her was boring. I thought I knew all about living, and I never did anything stupid or crazy."

Those words of his were seared into my memory. He smiled gently as he spoke.

"But now I simply enjoy my days with Hino. I truly feel like if there's something I can do for her with a little extra effort, then I want to do it. She surprises me and makes me see things in a new light. She makes me feel like I want to be a better person."

Up until a certain point, I thought Tooru and Maori were very different. But it was only a superficial contrast. I felt embarrassed. Humans have the ability to see the world with their heart, but I only saw it with my eyes. Once I looked with my heart, their similarities were obvious. No matter the situation, they were always thoughtful of others. They were able to understand other people's feelings, to take them into consideration.

I thought about that conversation with Tooru as I walked home with Maori after the picnic that day. I wasn't sure what had prompted her to ask me if I liked Tooru. All the same, her intentions came across. Even with amnesia, she had been considerate, worrying whether she was getting in the way of her friend's crush. My denial should have expelled that concern. I didn't let any of my inner turmoil show.

Spring break ended, and our third year of high school began. Due to her amnesia, Maori was transferred out of the advanced class, and the head third-year teacher arranged for her to join Tooru's class.

As long as he was there, I wasn't needed.

When she woke up every morning, she learned of her condition and read her journals and notebooks before going to school. Tooru would be in her class when she got there. He was her boyfriend, and unbeknownst to her, he knew about her amnesia. Tooru Kamiya, who tried to bring joy to her life every day.

Overwhelmed with studying for university entrance exams, I pretended not to notice my loneliness from being apart from Maori or my budding feelings for Tooru. Maori and I still texted and talked on the phone every day. We saw each other often at school. But instead of me, Tooru was always by her side.

When the three of us were together, we chatted like usual. Sometimes, in the middle of a conversation, Tooru would just stare, captivated, at her face. I could see the love in his eyes. Every time I saw it, my chest ached. I knew my own love had no outlet. But I should have been more careful. Because someone was right next to me, watching me watch him.

"Izumi...do you by chance have a crush on Tooru?"

It was the day after Golden Week when Maori asked me that for the second time. I knew that she and Tooru had been planning to go to the zoo over the break. They'd invited me, but I didn't want to get in their way, so I told them I had to study. After school, the day after vacation ended, the two of them came to my classroom to give me a souvenir from the zoo.

"Hino and I chose this for you because we thought you might like it. It's a handmade bookmark."

To be completely accurate, Tooru was the one who gave me the souvenir. He took the elegantly wrapped bookmark out of his bag and handed it to me. I hadn't expected to get a present.

"What? For me?"

"Yeah. Tooru was the one who saw it and thought you'd like it," Maori said.

"No, I… Okay, yes, I did."

"Why did you try to deny it? Are you shy?"

"No, I am not shy. By the way, Hino said these cookies from the zoo were really good, so I picked some up without telling her. I brought some tea in my thermos, too, so how about we eat them together?"

He'd not only made the Maori on the day of their date happy; he was also bringing today's Maori joy with his present. It had been a long time since the three of us talked, and we really enjoyed our conversation. That day, I realized that even I had a feminine side. It was the first time a guy had ever given me a present. It was just a small thing, a bookmark that probably cost a few hundred yen. But Tooru had picked it out for me.

I kept glancing at his face as the three of us talked. And my heart ached—it was a bittersweet feeling. After a while, he said he was going to the bathroom and left the classroom. Once he was safely out of earshot, Maori timidly said, "Hey, I was wondering…"

"What? Can you believe Kamiya kept those cookies secret from you?"

"Izumi…do you by chance have a crush on Tooru?"

Time froze.

Ideally, I shouldn't have paused, because in a way, I was confirming her suspicions. But a thought flitted across my mind. What would happen if I told her I liked him? What would happen if I said, *Yes, I do like him*? She would probably be surprised. She might think I was joking. Or she might think I meant I liked him as a friend. But if she did realize I meant it in a different way…she might smile sadly and say, *So you finally like someone*.

And then what would I do? Since they were a couple, would I say she didn't need to worry about me? Would she go along with that?

You're very important to me, too. So if you liked him…I would be worried I was getting in the way.

I recalled what she'd told me before. If I said I liked him, it might not just make her sad—it might cause something even worse to happen. I knew I wasn't overthinking. She was that kind of person. She was like Tooru. She put her friends' happiness before her own. Maori would tell herself that Tooru would be better off with me because of her amnesia…

In front of me, she would probably act like it was no big deal to break up with him. What would Tooru do then? Would he push back, insisting that he wanted to stay together? Probably not. In all likelihood, he would respect her decision, assuming she had her reasons for doing it. And…they would part ways. In the worst-case scenario, they would genuinely break up.

Then what would I do? If Tooru was single, would it be okay to tell him I liked him?

At that point, I realized something. My feelings for Tooru really were getting in the way. They only served to destroy Maori's happiness. In which case, they'd be better off not existing. They'd be better off disappearing. Fortunately, Maori couldn't retain memories. They didn't remain unless she wrote them in her journal.

"What? I'm so surprised, I froze for a second. Me, like Tooru? No way, that's impossible," I said, making a strong effort to smile.

"...Really?" she said, giving me a slightly searching look.

I repeated my answer from before, like I only saw the outer appearance of others. Like I was a shallow person. I reeled off those stale lines to convince Maori I had no feelings for Tooru.

But I didn't leave it at that. I couldn't.

"I hate to ask you this, Maori, but would you mind not writing down what you asked me today in your journal?"

"Why not? If I don't write it down, I might ask you again," she said, puzzled. I put on a faint smile and answered jokingly.

"That's fine, I'll just say the same thing again. If you write in your journal that you asked me if I like Kamiya...even though you know I have absolutely no interest in him, since he and I are friends, I would be so embarrassed if he ever read your journal, and it would be awkward. So, please? Just to make your best friend happy?"

If I didn't say that, she might have written down our conversation. This was the second time she'd asked. That was clearly unnatural. Once her memory was reset and she was reading her journals objectively, it might strike her as odd. Like she must have had a reason for asking me twice.

"Okay, I promise not to write it down. You know I can't say no to you," she said.

And she kept her promise. The next day, when I saw her, I said, "By the way, about the thing I asked you to do yesterday…" She gave me a genuinely confused look. She couldn't have possibly faked that reaction.

"Um, I'm sorry, Izumi. What did you ask me to do?"

"I'm getting behind on studying…"

After that, I promised myself I wouldn't make the same mistake again. When the three of us were together, I did my utmost not to focus on Tooru. I kept my conversations with him as short as possible without seeming unnatural. I didn't steal glances at him when he was looking the other way. I thought that would do the trick. Unfortunately…

Who was the poet who originally came up with that famous saying? It's included in all sorts of books and proverb dictionaries and websites listing famous quotes.

You can't hide love or coughs.

"Maybe I'm misreading this…but do you by chance have a crush on Tooru?"

"Izumi…do you like Tooru?"

"Hey, I was wondering, is Tooru your type?"

"…Sorry if this is a weird question, but do you…?"

No matter how many times I tried to redo the situation, Maori always seemed to notice my feelings. It wasn't that she was trying to warn me so that she could keep him for herself. She was asking because she simply, innocently wondered if she was getting in my way.

The problem was on my end. I shouldn't have been interested in him.

At the start of summer vacation, I completely stopped interacting with him. Sometimes, I hung out with Maori, but if Tooru was there, I stayed away. The previous summer, I'd felt lonely because we weren't hanging out as a group, but in the summer of our third year, I intentionally avoided hanging out as a threesome.

Maybe because he knew I was studying for university entrance exams, Tooru never mentioned it. When summer vacation ended, I ran into him in the hallway. I hadn't seen him in a long time. Pain and affection welled up within me, making my eyes sting.

"Hi, Izumi!"

But Maori was by his side. Of course she was. They were always together at school.

"Did you lose weight, Wataya?" Tooru asked after I'd said hello to Maori.

"...The summer heat has been getting me down. Anyway, how are things going with Maori?" I asked.

"Fine. We're getting along great."

"Glad to hear it. I'm on duty today in homeroom, so I'd better be going. Bye, Maori."

I smiled and left them. My mission was to reduce contact with Tooru to a bare minimum, while making sure it didn't seem unnatural to Maori. After summer vacation, things continued on without a hitch. I thought I'd be able to hide my feelings that way. But that fall, something completely unexpected happened. My feelings were entirely exposed to Maori.

2

As summer turned to fall, the first- and second-year students started to talk incessantly about the school festival. Our high school generally didn't put much energy into school events. Still, there was always a sports festival and a school festival, like they were part of the standard operating procedure. Since the school festival took place close to university entrance exams for third-year students, the first and second years handled most of the preparations.

The event only lasted one day, and it wasn't open to the public. There also weren't any stalls cooking or heating food, which would have required a notification to the health department. But some students looked forward to it anyway.

Maori was one of them. The night before the festival, when we talked on the phone, she seemed a little jealous of her tomorrow's self. That she would get to spend the whole day walking around the festival with Tooru.

The next morning as I was getting ready, her mother called me.

"I'm sorry to call so early," she said. "Maori has a bit of a fever and doesn't feel well. She's come to grips with her amnesia, and she's calm now…but I'm thinking of having her stay in bed today."

A few minutes later, Maori sent me a text.

Izumi?

What's up? How's your fever?

A "read" notification popped up right away. But no message followed. Just as I was thinking of calling her, a reply came.

Oh, good. I knew because I could see that we've been texting every day, but—

Yeah?

I've been getting on with life even with amnesia, haven't I? I've been going to school, and we're still friends, right?

I could tell she was feeling discouraged today as a consequence of her cold. She woke up in the morning feeling sick, but reality didn't stop because of that. She'd learned about her accident and memory loss and that nearly a year and a half had passed. It was only natural that she would feel anxious. I wanted to cheer her up.

Of course! Nothing has changed. Don't worry.

Okay...that's a relief.

You go to school every day. Just like your journal says, you seem to be enjoying life.

I read a little of it. I was so surprised. I have a boyfriend now?

Yeah, Kamiya, a guy who was in a different class from you last year. He's tall and thin. Sound familiar?

Vaguely. He's a nice guy, right? Not like my impression of him.

I smiled wryly. If Tooru hadn't been nice, a lot of things probably wouldn't have worked out. Maori might have felt anxious every day. She might not have managed to stay in school. I wouldn't have gotten a crush on him...

I hear you're sick today, so take it easy, okay? You don't have to be afraid of tomorrow. I know it will be another good day for you. There's nothing to worry about.

You're right. Today...I'll take it easy.

Good. I'll get in touch with Kamiya. Don't worry about anything, really.

Thanks, Izumi. Thanks to you, I think I'll be okay.

I read her text and closed the messaging app. Then I opened my email and sent a message to Tooru, who had an old flip phone. I told him Maori had a cold and was staying home but that her mood was stable.

Got it. Thanks, Wataya.

I read his reply, finished getting ready, and headed to school.

My last high school festival was beginning. Homeroom ended quickly, and the start of the festival was announced over the intercom. Since I was in the advanced class, some students stayed in the classroom studying or took their things to the library instead of going to the festival. I was planning on doing the same. Whether Maori was there or not, I intended to spend the day quietly studying in the library.

"Wataya?"

But someone stopped me on my way there. I turned around. Tooru was standing there alone. He walked down the hallway until he was right in front of me.

"Want to go to the festival together?" he asked.

I must have looked pretty surprised.

"What, why?"

"Why? Because today is the festival."

"I…don't need to go. Maori's not here, and you'd probably be more relaxed by yourself. Don't worry about me. Bye."

I turned around and started walking away. The hallway leading to the library was sunless and cold. The noise from the festival didn't reach here. It was quiet, so quiet…

Maybe that's why my heartbeat sounded so gratingly loud.

"Did I do something to make you hate me?" Tooru asked.

I stopped walking and faced him again. He was frowning, as though the situation troubled him. My heart refused to calm down. Along with the pain, something stirred and spread throughout my chest.

Tooru didn't really need to interact with me if Maori wasn't there. Both of us were good at spending time alone. He might as well kick back with a novel. But maybe because he thought I'd been acting strange, he made a point of seeking me out. He invited me to the festival and tried to cheer me up because we were friends.

For once, he was looking just at me, thinking only of me.

My heartbeat was deafening. I was hurting, I was suffering, and I was happy. For a moment, I couldn't speak.

Maori wasn't here. Maybe I could get away with it. I wouldn't tell anyone; I wouldn't leave any traces. Maybe it was okay to create a memory that belonged only to me and Tooru.

I gazed silently at Tooru. Then, for the first time in ages…I smiled at him.

"What are you talking about, Kamiya?"

He seemed surprised by my cheerful words and attitude. I burst out laughing and walked over to him.

"I'm sorry, I've been so nervous about exams that I've been kind of high-strung since summer. You didn't do anything, and I don't hate you."

How long had it been since I'd let down my guard around him? I had to be careful not to talk too fast out of pure happiness.

"Really? I guess that makes sense. I bet you're applying to a national university. The test sounds hard, especially with all those subjects."

"You're taking the public service exam, right? I heard that one has a lot of subjects, too."

"Yeah, but the exam was this summer, so it's over."

"No way. The civil service exam is that early? So you're free to take it easy now?"

"There are more tests down the road, but I'm free enough to have some fun today. How about you?"

He smiled at me. He was always a little mischievous like that when he talked to me. My heart trembled at the familiarity of our exchange. I realized I was happy and there was nothing I could do about it.

"I'm free enough to have some fun today, too," I said, matching his joking tone. "Since it's our last festival and all...I think I'll let you show me a good time."

Tooru and I were going to walk around the festival together as friends, just friends. That was the objective reality. Reality is stubborn. It doesn't change. But it didn't matter. I didn't care how he felt. I made up my mind to create my own special memory that day. I was sure the gods would forgive me. After all, it was just a little thing...

"So where should we go? Is there anything you want to see?"

"Let me put away my books and stuff first. We can decide where to go after that."

"Oh, sorry. You're right."

"Since you invited a lady to the festival, you'd better escort her properly," I teased before arranging to meet him by the entryway and heading back to my classroom.

"Ladies don't run down hallways," he shouted after me. I must have broken into a jog without realizing it.

"Shut up!" I shouted back, my voice as bouncy as my steps.

I quickly fixed up my hair and makeup before meeting Tooru at the entryway to head into the festival. He had dutifully fetched the festival pamphlet handed out in homeroom. We studied it before heading out.

Naturally, we were standing close together, but I pretended not to feel anything.

First, we went to buy some cotton candy so we could walk around eating it and feel like we were at a festival. Everyone else must have had the same idea because there was a long line by the stall in the courtyard. It only cost fifty yen, so we did rock-paper-scissors to decide who would treat the other. Even though I lost, Tooru insisted on paying when we got to the counter, saying, "I invited you, after all." Pleased and embarrassed, I jabbed him in the side with my elbow. Maybe it surprised him, because he gave me an odd look.

After that, he said there was something he wanted to see, so we walked over to the athletic field, cotton candy in hand. A flea market had been set up there, organized by the teachers and clubs. Items were displayed in messy rows. Judging by the old electronic devices mixed in, the teachers had clearly scoured their houses for stuff they couldn't otherwise get rid of.

Tooru went into housewife mode searching for deals, and I burst out laughing at how intense he was. He protested bashfully, and we joked around about it. This wasn't intimacy between a boy and a girl, but banter between friends who got along well. I smiled so much at the silly jokes that filled our casual conversation that my cheeks started to hurt.

I knew this would be painful to look back on in the future. It wasn't like the times we'd ended up together without Maori by chance. He and I were intentionally spending time together, and it would probably never happen again. It wasn't a date, but to me, it was. Since I knew this was my one and only chance, I wanted to enjoy it to the fullest. I wanted us to smile and laugh together.

Some of the clubs had set up stands, and I was curious about what the Literature Club was doing, so we went to take a look. A couple of their members were hovering restlessly in the room they were in, and copies of the club magazine were set out on a desk.

"I bet they'd be shocked if they found out you were Keiko Nishikawa's brother," I whispered to Tooru. He smiled shyly.

We picked up copies of the magazine and headed for the popcorn stand. We stopped by the ring toss and the haunted house, making the rounds. We had a good time together.

"Whew, I'm tired from laughing so much. Can we take a break?" I asked. I really was tired from laughing, so we slipped into an empty room being used as a rest area. No one else was there, so we kept bantering with each other.

"Kamiya, stop making me laugh!"

"You pick up everything I say and turn it into a joke!"

"I was good at volleyball in gym class, you know. I must be a gifted receiver."

"A gifted receiver? So you mean a telephone you got as a present?"

"What kind of present is that?"

We couldn't stop talking, so we decided to take a break by reading the magazines we'd picked up. About halfway through, I realized something.

"Do you write fiction, Kamiya? Your sister and your dad are both writers, aren't they?"

He looked up from his magazine with genuine surprise.

"You're right. I'm not sure why, but it's never occurred to me to write anything."

"Interesting. You don't want to?"

"Not now, at least. There are…other things I'd rather do one day."

Tooru always put his family and Maori first. He prioritized other people over himself. So it was a surprise to hear there was something he wanted to do.

"Really? What is it?"

"Please don't laugh. I'm kind of interested in photography," he said a bit reluctantly, like he was embarrassed to admit it.

Photography. He'd never mentioned that before. Maori might not have known, either.

"Of course I wouldn't laugh. But why photography?"

"Well…photos are like novels in that they take you to other places, right? Because of my family situation, I've never been able to travel much… Sometimes, I feel really drawn to photographs. I'll see a beautiful photo and imagine myself there, which makes me want to go somewhere myself and take pictures like that."

I was deeply impressed by Tooru's words. For various reasons, he had probably never been on a trip in his whole life. In a sense, the same was true for me. We knew nothing of the world beyond the place we belonged to. But photographs and novels took us to other worlds. Photos especially, since they were real. They opened windows to unknown places. I could see why he was drawn to that.

"If I told my family or Hino about it, they might take it too seriously," he went on bashfully. "I've never told anyone but you about this."

His smile and confession left me speechless. I was so happy. So happy that he had shared a secret just with me. He was telling a friend something he couldn't tell his family or his girlfriend. I was someone special to him.

But I couldn't let him guess what I was feeling. Instead, I made a joke.

"Hey, you could start taking pictures now. Didn't you say you were mostly done studying for the civil service exams? You have ideal subjects in me and Maori."

"I'm more interested in landscapes."

"But you have something more beautiful than a landscape right in front of you!"

He laughed.

"This is no laughing matter!" I said, pretending to get mad. He apologized. We joked around like that. But…something occurred to me, and it made my heart ache.

One day, Tooru would have the freedom and the money to buy a camera. He would probably use it to take pictures of Maori. My heart pounded quietly but powerfully. Before that happened, couldn't I have one thing? Before he took photos of Maori with a real camera? Just something simple, something silly—that was enough.

"Would you take a picture of me now, since we're at the festival and everything?" I said, like I was carrying on the joke. He raised his eyebrows slightly.

"Seriously? But I'm an amateur. Also, I don't have a camera on my phone."

"Then I'll lend you mine. That works, right?"

I opened the camera on my phone and handed it to him. I didn't intend to make him do it if he really didn't want to. But he took my phone with a strained smile and looked at the camera app with interest.

"Can I mess around with this?"

"Do whatever you want. It's not like you'll break it."

I showed him how to use it. He brushed his long, thin finger over the screen. He asked me some technical questions. When I asked how he knew that stuff, he said he'd been reading some photography books. I answered the best I could, and he started adjusting the settings.

"Here I go. Are you ready, Wataya?"

"Make sure I look pretty."

"You're pretty to start with, so that won't be a problem."

"I swear…"

I knew he was joking, but I couldn't help smiling. I heard the shutter click. Tooru was smiling. He lowered the phone and started reviewing the pictures, still grinning. Then his expression changed to one of surprise.

"What's wrong? Don't tell me I closed my eyes."

"No. It's just…it must be beginner's luck. I feel like they came out really good."

He handed me the phone, and I started looking through the photos. Like him, I was dumbfounded. In the pictures…I looked so happy, I hardly recognized myself.

I was supposed to be cold, someone whose thoughts nobody could guess. But the person in those pictures was different. I looked overjoyed to be with the person outside the frame. You could tell from the warm expression on my face. I seemed different than I did in the usual pictures I took with Maori. So this was how I looked with Tooru?

Calming my trembling heart, I made a joke as usual.

"Don't you think my face looks puffy?"

Tooru just smiled quietly and said nothing.

After lunch, we checked out the Band Club and Theater Club exhibits in the gym and peeked into the crowded stalls together. We bantered the whole time. The festival ended with a performance by the

Pop Music Club and other volunteers in the gym. Neither of us were the type to stand in the front row of a crowd and go wild. Instead, we went to the open, empty school rooftop and listened to the distant music.

It was really fun.

It took me back to when I was six or seven, when my parents still got along. One weekend, the three of us went to an amusement park. We were all so happy. In the evening, my dad put me on his shoulders as we walked back to the parking lot. He was a taciturn, diligent person, not the type to do things like that. It was the first time I'd ever ridden on his shoulders. I hugged his head gently. My mom was a bit worried, but my dad said something to her, and she smiled. I remember very clearly how content she looked.

My father was busy at work and often couldn't play with me, but I thought he looked handsome and cool in his suit. My mother was young and elegant, and her job as a designer set her apart from most people. I adored them both. When the three of us were smiling together, I had a place where I felt secure. I could simply be happy. A normal kid, free of worries.

As I moved up in elementary school, that secure place disappeared. My dad was too busy with work to come home as much. At a certain point, my mom must have given up on him, because she began pouring herself into work, too. My parents stopped interacting with each other, and when they had to, they fought.

I started junior high. While crying, I tried to mediate between them. They had been so happy together. What had I missed? What had I failed to see? I started to feel afraid of people because I couldn't see their true selves.

For reasons related to my father's job, they didn't divorce. My mother agreed to this. But they both started seeing other people, and they separated. I believed in them less and less, and I mourned the loss of something important to me. But I avoided thinking about it, because I knew when I did, I would become endlessly sad.

Still…I was heartbroken. I had lost the place where I could feel safe. But when I was with Tooru, somewhere within me, I felt at ease. There, all I had to do was innocently experience the world. All I had to do was smile, enjoy myself, and be happy. I was able to be an ordinary girl, free of worries. I was able to forget all my sadness and anxiety and simply be myself.

Is that what love is?

I was too embarrassed to tell anyone these things, but when I was alone with Tooru, that's what I thought about.

"Thanks for asking me to hang out today, Kamiya. I had a good time."

We were sitting on a bench on the roof of the school, gazing at the sky and listening to the performance.

"Thanks for going along with it. I had fun as well."

I looked over at him. He was smiling gently. To keep my love from spilling out, I flashed him an amused grin, the kind a friend would make. "It wasn't just fun. Today I learned a secret about you."

"A secret?"

"Photography."

"Oh…that. But what about you, is there anything you want to do?"

"Me?"

"I've never heard you talk about it. Do you want to write a novel?"

I hadn't expected him to ask me the same question, and it got me thinking. I liked novels, but I'd never considered writing one. In junior high, my family situation didn't leave mental space for that. And high school was dominated by my studies and Maori's amnesia. Maori had drawing. Tooru had photography. And I...

"I've never thought about writing anything, either. But maybe I could. When things calm down, maybe I'll give it a try. I'll win the new writer prize while I'm still in university, and everyone will praise me as a beautiful young authoress. I'll do talk events with your sister and stuff."

Although I'd been joking around, Tooru smiled placidly.

"I'll be first in line to get your signature."

"Hey, at least make fun of me for calling myself a beautiful young authoress! If you don't, I'll be embarrassed!"

"Why? It's true. You're pretty."

"...You sure have a knack for saying embarrassing things with a straight face. I thought the same thing when you took my picture this morning. I'd forgotten that about you."

He got all flustered, which made me smile. I wondered if I was making the same face I'd made in those pictures. But maybe it was okay, just for today, because Maori wasn't there.

I wanted to smile because I was happy and because I was with Tooru.

I thought about that as we joked around some more. The concert in the gym ended. I checked the time on my phone and realized that the school festival was almost over.

"I guess it's time to go back to class," I said.

"Is it already that late? It went by so fast."

We grinned at each other and stood up from the bench. I glanced at the door leading inside. Just then, I glimpsed something move on the other side of the glass. For a split second, I thought I saw long black hair flying.

"What's wrong, Wataya?" Tooru asked warily.

"Hmm? Oh, nothing," I answered, walking toward the door.

Someone must have been about to come out onto the roof but turned around when they saw someone else there. I started to ascend the short staircase leading up to the door, planning to go back inside. Suddenly, the glimpse of long black hair made me think of Maori.

"By the way," I said, stopping and turning around. Tooru was right behind me. When I realized he was there…it happened. My lips inadvertently brushed his cheek as I turned my head. I think we both widened our eyes at the same moment. It was a complete accident.

"Sorry," I said, turning my face away like it was nothing.

"No, I'm sorry," he apologized. He knew it was no more than a coincidence, and he didn't act weird about it.

"Anyway, I was going to say," I went on, pretending to be calm. I was going to bring up Maori's amnesia, so I looked around to make sure no one was there before lowering my voice to a whisper. "About Maori… I think you know this, but it would probably be better not to tell her about today. I don't know what tomorrow's Maori will think about it, but she might feel sad if she knew the two of us had so much fun together at the festival."

Maybe because I'd brought up her amnesia, his expression grew serious. A moment later, though, it softened.

"Thank you for always putting Hino first," he said.

"Why should you thank me?"

"Why not? I can be grateful to you."

We smiled at each other again, then walked up the short staircase and went inside. After we went down the stairs leading to the lower floor, Tooru said he needed to go to the staff room, and we split up.

"Well, Wataya, thanks for today."

"Thank you, too."

"Don't study too hard."

"I won't."

He walked off toward the staff room. I silently watched his back. After he disappeared from view, I remembered my lips brushing his cheek. I softly brought my finger to my mouth. I had a hopeless crush on him. But tomorrow, I would have to put it out of my mind. In front of Maori, I had to keep my distance from him.

"Izumi…"

Just then, someone murmured my name. And it wasn't just anyone. I recognized that familiar voice. I jerked my head around. There she was, with her beautiful, long black hair—Maori, smiling half-heartedly, in the hallway.

It took me a few seconds to register what was happening. She was supposed to be at home with a fever, but instead she was here in front of me.

"Huh? …Maori? What about your cold?" I asked, hiding how shaken I felt. She looked like she was going to cry.

"…I slept for a little while, and I felt better. So…"

Her next words wrung my heart.

"I wanted to see you. When I read yesterday's journal, it said you were going to study during the school festival, but… I thought maybe we could go around together. I thought I'd surprise you, so I came to school after lunch, and…"

She'd come just to see me. But I hadn't even noticed her there. Not only that…

"I'm sorry, Izumi. Was the person you were with just now Tooru

Kamiya? I looked at his picture this morning, and I vaguely remember seeing him before my accident."

She was apologizing even though she hadn't done anything wrong. I could tell she was desperately forcing herself to smile as she asked me if it was him. I explained the situation with equal desperation.

"Yes, that was him. Your boyfriend, Tooru Kamiya. I told him you had a fever today. He wanted to go to the festival with you, but he must have thought I looked worn out from studying, and…so as a sort of break, we decided to check out the festival. He and I are friends. I said he must be lonely because you weren't there. And so…"

"Izumi…do you like Tooru Kamiya?"

"What, why? He's just a friend."

"I saw the two of you walking around the festival. Not just that. I knew I shouldn't have; I knew I should have stopped…but I saw you talking on the roof, too. You looked happy. My, well, my yesterday is different from everyone else's…so I can see certain things. You were looking at him like you cared about him a lot."

I was shocked speechless. I'd wondered why she was always able to notice my feelings for Tooru so quickly. Now I knew. To Maori, I was the Izumi from before her accident. I must have changed enough that the discrepancy between my two selves was enough to tip her off. Especially when I was with Tooru.

"I'm really getting in your way, aren't I? I'm sorry," she said. She smiled, but she couldn't hide the tears that slid down her eyes. She turned around, hesitated for a second, then started running.

"Maori… Maori!"

I ran after her. If I didn't catch up with her, I knew it would be bad. I would be making her sad over and over. That was the one thing I wanted to prevent no matter what.

I cared about her tremendously. I knew she was better for Tooru than I was. I knew they were truly in love.

"I'm the one who's getting in the way!" I shouted down the empty hallway. Fortunately, no one else was around. No one to give me nasty looks for yelling.

I saw her react to my words. She slowed down, then finally stopped and looked at me. I ran up to her, panting.

"Listen to me, Maori. I'll explain everything!"

"Izumi."

"I…I do like Kamiya."

I said it. I went and said it. I told her. I confessed.

But I couldn't let my words and feelings stop there.

"But above all else…I care about the two of you. You, and Kamiya when he's with you. And you when you're with Kamiya."

I hadn't thought up those words in advance—they came naturally in the moment. And I was struck by them. It wasn't just Tooru. I cared just as much about Maori and about the two of them together.

When I said it, something strange happened. Maori looked even more startled. As I wondered why, my vision blurred. Then I realized— I was crying. That was why she was surprised.

The tears stung…but they were also warm.

For the first time, I cried for a reason other than being sad.

I was always disappointed in myself, always giving up on myself. I thought I was cold, someone whose thoughts no one could guess. I never thought of the things I did as pure or beautiful.

Nothing like Tooru did, loving someone else more than himself.

Or like Maori, fighting against despair and still managing to believe in the future.

I didn't think anything so beautiful existed inside of me. But in that moment, I realized that in a certain way, I was like them. I was forced to realize it.

I cared about Tooru. I cared about Maori. I cared even more about the two of them together.

They meant more to me than my own self. That wasn't a lie. It was the one pure, beautiful thing inside of me.

I wiped my tears away and continued on the best I could.

"I don't think today's you knows Kamiya very well yet. But you really are a great couple. Just read your journal and you'll see. You'll see how much he loves you. How much he treasures you. How much you…care for him. I haven't read your journal, but I know that much."

Maori had clearly changed since she'd started dating Tooru. She still lived with the despair of having anterograde amnesia, but she enjoyed her life. I knew her better than anyone. That was why I was so sure.

"The two of you mean more to me than my own self."

Words are always vague, no matter whether you say too much or too little; they never really convey what you're thinking. Ambiguous signs. Fragmented emotions. Still, I hoped my feelings got through to her. I wanted her to understand.

"But Izumi…you like him, don't you? Are you okay with this? Isn't it painful? I have amnesia, and you're more…"

"Kamiya isn't the type to care about that kind of thing. Even if he knew about your amnesia, he would never dislike you for it. If that wasn't the case…I wouldn't have fallen for him. No matter what condition you're in, he loves you and only you."

I was still keeping it a secret that Tooru knew about Maori's amnesia. Nevertheless, I desperately tried to convey his love for her. And…

"That's why… That's why he'll never be interested in me. It's a common story. There's nothing I can do about it."

When I accepted that, the reality of the situation slid easily into my consciousness. My feelings were unrequited, and nothing would come of them. It didn't matter if the two of them broke up. He would still love her alone.

"And…yes, it hurts. If I'm being honest, it was painful keeping this from you. Because I couldn't tell anyone how I felt. Because I thought it was wrong for me to like him."

I had been suppressing my own feelings by telling myself they would only get in the way and cause trouble for Maori and Tooru.

But…maybe I'd been wrong. Maybe I could care for him in a way that didn't interfere. Maybe I could still hold on to these feelings, without wanting him to reciprocate them.

That was all right, wasn't it? To be able to feel that way about him?

I wanted to ask Maori.

The tears that I thought I'd wiped away kept falling miserably as I went on talking.

"But I was able to tell today's you. Is it…all right…if I like him? I promise I won't cause any trouble for the two of you. So, so…is it okay if I keep on liking him?"

When I asked her this, she started crying, too. I knew why. Because she was kind. She was crying because she was thinking about how I must feel. She hugged me before answering.

"It's okay, Izumi. It's okay to cherish your own feelings. I'm sorry to put you through this. But…thank you. And I'm sorry. Really, thank you."

For a few more minutes, she kept hugging me and crying.

We skipped homeroom that day and talked on the roof instead. Some things are more important than school rules.

Without feeling any guilt or sorrow, I asked Maori not to write anything that happened today in her journal. My request confused her somewhat, but after I explained my reasons, she agreed. There's a limit to what words can capture. If she wrote about today, we wouldn't know how those words would affect her future selves.

For instance, if she wrote *Izumi likes Tooru Kamiya, but more than that, she cares about me and him, so she wants us to be together*, it might weigh on her in the future. In which case, it would be better not to write anything at all. Better if nothing changed.

"I think I was acting unnaturally before today," I told her. "I was trying to convince you that something real didn't exist. That's unnatural, right? And I was suffering for no reason. But today I told you the truth…and it was such a relief when you said it was okay to cherish my own feelings."

True to my words, I beamed radiantly at her. It was probably easier to pretend things that didn't exist did. But doing the opposite was harder. Things that exist inevitably have a presence, a mass. If you deny that, all kinds of contradictions arise. I learned that from this experience.

I liked Tooru Kamiya. That was okay. It was okay that nothing would come of my feelings, because I realized there were things I valued more than my one-sided crush.

I resigned myself without any lingering regret. And I felt like I'd be okay. I was sure I'd be able to go on being friends with Maori and Kamiya just like before.

Maori kept apologizing, but she had nothing to say sorry for. All I felt toward her was gratitude, and I told her so.

"Thank you, Maori. I was able to meet Kamiya because of you. And…I was able to experience having a crush for the first time in my life. I finally fell for someone."

She was silent for a while. I could imagine the myriad emotions swirling around within her. Regret toward me, anxiety about the future, all sorts of things. But out of every single feeling, she chose to focus on the most positive one.

"Wow, I really want to meet Tooru Kamiya as soon as I can. And…I want to see how I feel when I meet him."

She smiled at me.

"To be honest, after I woke up today, I didn't even care if tomorrow came or not. But now…I'm kind of looking forward to it. I'm not afraid to go to sleep. I have you, and this guy Tooru Kamiya who you like."

Obviously, I didn't tell Tooru what had transpired between me and Maori. I also tried not to think about it too much. I figured that was the least I could do, considering I'd asked Maori to forget about it.

The following day, Maori came to school seeming just like she always did. She didn't show any sign of having written down what happened the day before, and nothing seemed unnatural. She looked like she was having fun talking to Tooru.

"Hi, Izumi."

"Hey, Wataya."

I was okay with seeing him by then. I was able to act normal.

"Hey. Getting along like two peas in a pod, I see."

"Izumi, you're starting to sound like an old man," Maori said.

"Sometimes a geezer possesses her body," Tooru added.

"How dare you say that to a beautiful woman like me!"

They meant so much to me. I'd found something in life more valuable to me than myself. These two humans. I prayed that I would be able to be with them forever and ever.

Winter, the season of intense studying, began. In spring, I got into my first-choice university. Tooru was hired by the city hall in the neighboring district, and although Maori still had amnesia, she graduated from high school. We laughed together a lot. We spent spring break together. But that spring, something happened that could never be undone.

"I found out my heart might not be very strong, and…"

One day after the three of us hung out, Tooru and I went on a walk without Maori. That was when he told me this, his expression serious. Although I was surprised, I managed to hold myself together. But when I learned that he'd collapsed the day before, and that his mother had died of heart disease, and that he'd had various tests done as a child, I began to panic.

"Interesting. Um, if there's anything I can do, please don't hesitate to ask," I managed to say. I cared about him, and I wanted to support him.

"In that case…and I'm only saying *if* something happens, and the chances of that are basically zero. I just want to ask you while it's on my mind. I'm not saying this is going to happen to me, but people do die abruptly sometimes."

Maybe I should have never offered to help. I never guessed that he would ask me to do something so heartbreaking.

"If I die, I want you to erase me from Hino's journal."

In that moment, I was speechless; all words used as a means of communication vanished from my mind. After I somehow managed to retrieve them, I tried to turn what he'd said into a joke. I tried to do what I always did, which was to make light of things and laugh about them. But I couldn't do it. Tooru was serious.

"Wh-what are you talking about?"

So I resisted. Maybe I thought that by resisting, I could prevent that reality from happening.

"This is important," he said.

"I don't want to do that. You should do it yourself."

"You're right. I should. I'm sorry to ask something like this from you. But I want you to listen."

And then he explained, kindly and calmly. Since he'd never met Maori before she lost her memory, if he died, as long as he wasn't in her journal, it would be possible to make it like it had never happened.

He was worried about her mental state. On the off chance that something did happen to him, Maori would grieve for him. She would grieve every day. He was right, but I couldn't easily agree to his request. Even though my first crush was asking me to do it, Tooru, who I cared so much about, it wouldn't have been right for me to simply say yes.

In the end, though, he smiled and said, "I'm sorry to bring this up."

After that, I'm certain he said, "I'd better get going. See you later."

See you later. As if we would meet again. That's what he said. But…

The following night, he died suddenly from heart failure.

Sorrow and death are as natural as air in this world. Why did I think the two had nothing to do with me? I should have been familiar with sadness. How could I have thought death was unrelated to my life?

After Tooru died, I ultimately decided to do what he had asked me to. I removed all mention of him from Maori's journal. More accurately, since simply erasing him would have created a sense of incongruity, I had his sister help me edit the journals, substituting incidences of Tooru with me.

That wasn't all. I worked with Maori's parents to convince her that she'd always written her entries on her computer rather than in notebooks. We also replaced her phone because the old one had photos of Tooru and messages from him on it.

All of this was to fulfill Tooru's last wish. To protect Maori's heart—Maori, who Tooru had loved and cared for so deeply.

And so…his very existence vanished from within her.

3

I sat on a campus bench, the autumn wind blowing around me, thinking about Maori's life in high school and Tooru's request. About those days when I didn't even call him by his first name.

I was holding one of Maori's handwritten journals from high school—one of the real ones. Tooru was in it. They had laughed together every day. Hard and sad things must have happened now and then, but there were never any problems between the two of them.

Maori had Tooru, and Tooru had Maori.

Even though Maori suffered from anterograde amnesia, as long as she had Tooru and her journal full of happy memories, she was able to keep on living and believing in the future.

Until that day.

I wasn't sure if I should do this or not, but I decided to write about what happened to organize my thoughts.

My boyfriend, Tooru Kamiya, is dead. My past selves have described Tooru Kamiya in other entries, so please read those.

They said the cause of death was sudden heart failure. Kamiya's mother died of heart disease, and they said he might have inherited it.

I didn't know that people could just suddenly die.

I only know about him from what's written in my journal. I barely remember what he looks like.

Even so, when I learned that he had died, I couldn't stop crying.

A little while ago, I was at the wake with Izumi. I saw Tooru Kamiya lying in his coffin.

The person who made my past selves so happy had stopped moving.

I still can't make sense of it. I'm just sad, sad, so endlessly sad.

Every time I reread my past journal entries, the sadness wells up in me. I'm in there. Kamiya is in there. On every page, he and I are smiling.

I'm not trying to make my future self sad. Maybe I shouldn't be writing this entry, or if I write it, maybe I should tear it out and throw it away.

But today's self will only exist once. None of my other selves can take their place.

That's why I made up my mind to leave a record of today in my journal. Future selves, I'm sorry. Forgive me for leaving this journal entry behind.

Kamiya. I want to be with you. I want to see you and talk with you.

You're good at brewing black tea, I hear. Will you make me a cup? I want to know all about you. I didn't just want you to support me. I wanted to support you, too.

I want to be with you.

But I can't, can I? I'm so lonely. So sad.

Maori was in shock from Tooru's death. After that, she had to face two absurd realities every morning: her own amnesia and his death. She began to grow weaker. Her parents and I had heard that depression could be a complication of anterograde amnesia, and we worried that might be happening to her.

I considered removing the mention of Tooru's death from her

journals and making up another reason for his absence. But that would only be a temporary solution. Worse, it would go against his last wish.

"If I die, I want you to erase me from Hino's journal."

Two days before his death, he had collapsed, and one day before his death, he had asked that of me.

I hardly had any interactions with Hino before she lost her memory. So...if I die, as long as I'm not in her journal, we can make it like it never happened.

I'm certain he didn't want to die. He only said that to me out of an abundance of caution, because his own mother had passed suddenly from heart disease. But his request was cruel. Normally, people try to leave behind traces of themselves when they die. They have a powerful desire to leave proof that they once lived. But Tooru wanted the opposite. He wanted to erase all trace of his existence from his loved one's memory. He thought only of her.

"I think it might be possible. But are you okay with that?" I asked him that day. He smiled sadly.

"I think I'll be okay with it."

The next night, he left the world of the living.

I agonized over what to do, but in the end, I decided to carry out his wish. Together with his sister and Maori's parents, I erased him from her journals. I kept her real journals, binders, and old phone at my place.

Once all traces of Tooru were gone, Maori gradually recovered. She wrote new journal entries on her computer, drew every day, and lived a quiet life, waiting to recover from her amnesia.

She forgot Tooru completely. It was like he had never existed. But unlike Maori, I couldn't erase him. My first crush. The first guy I ever liked. And now he was dead.

But as the days and months passed, I felt like I was coming to terms with his death. That's what it meant to go on living.

But…even if a person comes to terms with death, how can they come to terms with the unrequited feelings they had for someone who died?

I spent my first year of university trying to figure that out. I tried to find someone new to like, but I couldn't. I was stuck on my first crush, I guess. I didn't think anyone could replace Tooru.

That continued into my second year. I knew I couldn't go on like that. I had to forget him. I just didn't know how.

I…like you.

That's where I was when I met Naruse. His interest in me was almost blinding, and although I tried to turn him down, I made the mistake of accepting on one condition.

"I'll date you, but under one condition. Don't fall in love with me. Can you promise me that?"

Playing at romance should have been enough. A temporary, superficial, coincidental, transient, make-believe love.

Hello. I found you.

You're pretty attractive yourself.

Thank you for today. I had a good time. I'm looking forward to the aquarium.

But in a way, Naruse was similar to Tooru, and I began to have feelings for him in spite of myself. That made me afraid of him. I felt like he would overwrite my memories of Tooru. The places I'd been with

Tooru, the things I wanted to do with him, the things I wanted to see. I felt like Naruse's presence would inescapably erase all those things.

I was conflicted. I wanted to forget Tooru, but I also desperately didn't want to. And I ended up hurting Naruse because of it.

Maybe I'd be better off if I could forget everything, like Maori. But that wasn't because Maori desired it. She inexorably forgot the things she wanted to remember. She was made to forget memories—of Tooru Kamiya, the person she loved.

As fall turned into winter, one month after I had sat on that bench reminiscing about the past, Maori found a sketchbook full of drawings of Tooru in her room. About a year and a half had passed since his death.

"Do you know who this is?" she asked me one afternoon at a café, showing me the sketchbook.

I'd thought I removed all trace of Tooru—journals, photographs, even drawings. I didn't realize that she had hidden sketches of him behind a bookshelf in her room.

For the first time, I told her the truth. That she used to have a boyfriend named Tooru Kamiya. That his support was the reason she'd managed to graduate from high school. That one day, he had suddenly died. Not just that. I told her that following his last wish, I had erased all trace of him from her journal.

She was shocked. I was afraid our friendship would end that day. But that wouldn't have been like her. She forgave us for what we had done. Although she was surprised, she smiled, with great effort, I'm sure, and told me she was grateful that we had tried to protect her.

After talking to her parents, I returned her the original journals. She read them and began trying to learn about the boyfriend she had forgotten for so long. She even contacted Tooru's sister in Tokyo. It seems his sister had expected to get that call one day. She came to our town, and I introduced the two of them. Maori asked about Tooru and seemed to gain some direction in her life.

Tooru had wanted her to forget him completely and regain her own life. There was no need to remember past sorrows. But Maori chose to face his death, even as she went on living. She chose to remember him. She vowed that one day she would remember everything.

But as for me…

4

The same day that Tooru's sister met Maori, she invited me to dinner at the hotel where she was staying.

Immediately after Tooru's death, she and I had discussed whether to erase him from Maori's journals. Afterward, we worked together to carry out our decision. In part because we had made this difficult choice together, a bond similar to friendship formed between us. At least, I thought it had. But like Tooru, I didn't want to get in the way of her career as an Akutagawa Prize–winning author, and it had been a long time since we met in person.

"Hello, Izumi. It's good to see you."

"The pleasure is mine. I've been following your work."

She had reserved a private room so we could talk more easily. In response to my stiff greeting, Tooru's beautiful sister smiled modestly.

"You don't have to be so formal. Anyway, I haven't been doing that much."

"I don't think that's true. I saw the movie, and it was great. I loved the book, too. And, well, I had a question about it…"

That night, I wanted to ask her for advice about how to come to terms with my feelings for Tooru. But there was something else I was dying to know first.

"The book that the movie was based on, did you write it after Tooru died?"

She must have guessed what I was getting at, because she looked me in the eye and said, "…I thought you might be the only one who noticed. I put a little of him into that novel."

One of the characters was a photographer in his twenties. He appeared in the movie, too. He seemed cold at first, but in reality, he cared more deeply than anyone else about his family, friends, and partner.

Tooru's sister was the only person I had told about his interest in photography. It was when I was checking over the journals that she had typed and rewritten, replacing him with me in Maori's entries.

"I wonder if there was anything Tooru wanted to do in life," she had mumbled. I hesitated but decided to tell her.

"Um…there was something he said he'd never told Maori or his family."

When I first read the novel, I wasn't sure if the character was based on Tooru, since his age and other things about him were slightly different. But when I reread the book and then saw the character on screen, I knew. It was definitely Tooru. Having many possible paths to choose from, Tooru pursued what he wanted in life. I only realized it in the second half of the movie. In spite of myself, I started crying.

"So it was Tooru."

"Yes."

Maybe in her own way, his sister had channeled her pain and sadness into her art. He had respected her very much, and she had cared for him deeply.

"Actually…I've been struggling with something related to Tooru. Would it be all right if I talked to you about it?" I asked, broaching the topic. She smiled kindly.

"Of course. You might laugh at me for saying this, but…sometimes, I think of you as my little sister. So please, tell me anything."

I'd had no idea she thought of me like that. Choked up with gratitude, I could hardly speak. But I made myself continue, trying to express my thoughts and feelings as honestly as possible. She listened intently, and when I was done, she tried to lighten the mood with a joke.

"Tooru sure was a lucky guy, to have two cute girls care so much about him."

"I'm not cute!"

She smiled at me as I hurried to counter the compliment. Then she said a little sadly, "And you still feel that way toward him, don't you?"

In the space of a second, my whole world went still. I'd been trying not to see the truth all this time, because I knew it was meaningless for those feelings to continue existing. They led nowhere. But perhaps I needed to acknowledge them. I still liked Tooru. He was the only one I liked.

"Maybe you're right."

"He was your first crush, yes?"

"…Yes. I…tried hard to forget him. I forced myself to date someone else. But I think I knew from the start that it wouldn't go well. In the end, I broke up with him, only thinking of myself."

"Ah…that sounds hard."

"What do you think I should do? How can I forget about Tooru? How can I overcome the grief?"

I always pretended not to notice my sadness. I've been like that since my parents' marriage fell apart. But when I said those words, I realized. I felt it keenly. Maybe I'd been depressed ever since Tooru died. Maybe I still was. As I stared at the table, his sister continued on hesitantly.

"If you're suffering because you can't forget Tooru…maybe the first step is trying to forget about yourself."

I looked up. She smiled, lightening the dark mood I'd created. Like me, she was in her twenties, but she had experienced so much. Her advice would never have occurred to me.

"Forget myself?"

"Yes. For example, is there something you want to do?"

"Yes."

She looked surprised, probably by how quickly I responded, and then her expression grew kind again.

"Having a goal makes life simple. If there's something you want to do, maybe you should try pouring yourself into it to the point that you forget yourself. Time will pass. All kinds of things will slip steadily into the past. Maybe you'll even forget some of the things you didn't think you could forget."

"A goal…," I mumbled. My voice was weak, but from where I sat buried in death and sorrow, the word sounded so distant. I'd heard about goals when I was little, but I'd nearly forgotten the word existed.

"By the way, what is it that you want to do? You don't have to tell me, but I'd love to know," she said as I sat there with my heart quietly trembling.

"I…want to try writing a novel."

After I said it, I felt ridiculous for even suggesting the idea as a total novice. Lots of people must have told her they wanted to write a book. She probably felt uncomfortable every time.

"What kind of novel?" she asked. Far from looking offended, she was cheerfully egging me on. Her smile brought out something locked away at the bottom of my heart.

"If you don't mind…I'd like to write about Tooru as best I can."

I'd tried it once but stopped before I finished. But I figured this was my only chance to bring it up, so I plunged ahead.

"Maybe it's a contradiction to write about him if I'm trying to forget him. But I want to try, partly to sort out my own feelings. And maybe submit it for a prize, or…"

I wanted his sister to read my novel. She knew Tooru better than I did, and I also respected her as a novelist. I couldn't even express how much her words had helped me. When I felt isolated, the ideas and words in her novels had given me immeasurable courage. But I couldn't show someone like her a poorly written novel. That was why I was thinking of submitting it to the literary contest she was a judge for. I'd polish it up and then have her read it.

But I wasn't sure about saying that to her directly. I didn't even know if I could finish it. The deadline was only three months away. More than anything, I worried that she wouldn't like a novel about her own brother.

"I can't wait to read it."

Instead, she smiled yet again. She even understood what I hadn't been able to say and responded calmly and impartially.

"I look forward to the day when I receive your novel, because I think you can write. It will be completely unique to you."

5

Fall became winter, and according to the calendar, it was already December. A lot happened during the time between spring and summer, and summer and fall. I felt like I hadn't achieved anything, but I knew I'd grasped something important. If I knew anything for sure, it was that I had a goal. I wanted to finish my novel about Tooru and enter it in the writing contest his sister was judging so she could read it.

"When we tell others about our sadness and pain, the meaning behind those feelings changes," Tooru's sister had said before I went home the night we had dinner. "We're able to gain a little distance. Always make sure you have someone you can talk to. Like…me, for example."

"Really, you don't mind? For someone like me to go to you…"

"Like I said earlier, I think of you as a younger sister. I'm sorry for not realizing how much pain you were in. From here on out, I'll be here for you."

After that, she started texting and calling me now and then, so it was easier for me to talk to her about things. Her warmth touched me. I wished she were my real sister. But I wondered how she would feel about that. Would she really want me as one?

No, I wasn't good enough. I wasn't the kind of person she could feel proud of yet.

Until recently, I had assumed that I was living my own life. But it was possible that I hadn't taken a single step forward since Tooru died. All I could think of was him. All I cared about was him. I'd even carelessly hurt the freshman who was interested in me.

That's when it hit me. I, more than anyone, was a prisoner of his death. When I realized that, I felt like I was able to truly rest for the first time in ages.

Maybe my life was finally beginning. No—I was the one who had to start it. That was another reason I wanted to lose myself in working toward my goal. I wanted to test myself. But now that I'd set my goal, there was something I had to do. Apologize to Naruse. I'd treated him horribly. I'd tried to forget Tooru in the completely wrong way and ended up pulling him into my problems. I'd hurt him so easily, without a second thought for his feelings.

I hadn't talked to him since we went to the aquarium. Since I felt so awkward, I'd avoided seeing him on campus since summer break ended. It was winter now, and I was still doing it.

"Naruse? You didn't hear? He's taking the semester off. I heard he ended the lease on his apartment, too."

Our mutual friend, the guy in my year who'd gone to high school with him, told me that the week after I had dinner with Tooru's sister. I'd asked him about Naruse because I thought it was odd that I hadn't seen him around campus in so long.

"Taking the semester off…really?"

I hadn't expected that. He didn't know why he'd left, which worried me. Was it because of me? Had I hurt him that badly?

I thanked him and screwed up my courage to send Naruse a message.

I heard you're taking time off school.

There was no "read" notification or a response. But that night, he wrote back.

Good to hear from you, Wataya. Thank you for your message. I'm…taking time off for some personal reasons.

I was relieved by his gentle reply and realized how nervous I'd been. I was prepared for him to hate me, but he didn't seem to hold any ill will toward me. I wondered what his "personal reasons" were, but I didn't want to pry, in case it had to do with his family. Still somewhat nervous, I tested the waters with a simple question.

Ah. Are you doing okay?

Yes, I'm fine. Things are tough, but I'm getting by.

What are you doing these days?

Working all the time.

He took off school to work? Something must have happened with his family after all. I started to worry that the end of our relationship had been the start to a string of bad luck. I was about to apologize and ask what had happened when he texted.

Uh, Wataya? I'm really happy that we're talking again.

I stared at his message. Then another one came.

I'm so glad I met you.

But everything I did to you was horrible.

That's not true. You were out of my league from the start.

Once again, I was painfully aware of how kind he was. Pure, humble, and unselfish…

I don't have anything to offer.

All the same, he sent me this painfully sad message. I wanted to tell him it wasn't true, but another text cut off my opportunity before I could finish typing.

How about you? How are you doing?

Me? Same as always. Going to class, helping my mom with work sometimes.

But there was something else, too. I decided to tell him.

Also, I'm writing a novel.

Really, a novel?

Yeah. I'm thinking of submitting it to a contest. Don't tell anyone, okay?

There was a pause, like he was trying to decide how to respond.

I won't. Thank you for telling me your secret.

I smiled at his conscientious response. I was about to reply when he texted again.

Oh, sorry. I have to get back to work.

I'd wanted to apologize. But now I realized that was simply because I wanted to make myself feel better. If I apologized at this late date, he would probably just worry about me. Maybe I was to live with how I'd treated him. I shouldn't let myself off the hook so easily.

Sorry to take up your break time. Thanks, I texted.

Take care. It's getting cold.

I will. You take care, too.

Thank you. Let's talk again sometime.

That was the end of our exchange. As I stared at his last message, it hit me that six months ago, he'd been right next to me, but I'd pushed him away. Now I was alone again. Everyone walks alone. Not just me.

Christmas was approaching, but I ignored the festive mood in town and attended class. I continued to work on my novel so I could submit it to the contest.

There were two categories: short stories and novellas. Both were literary fiction and had relatively short page limits. I figured the first step was to finish a draft. Through trial and error, I managed to complete it by the end of the year. It wasn't great, but I still felt slightly excited to have written my first work of fiction. When I reread it from the beginning, though, I realized I could never submit it as it was. I rewrote it from page one.

It was winter break, and I lost all sense of time, skipping lunch and even dinner, forgetting to sleep, just sitting all day at my computer writing my novel. Before I knew it, three days had passed, and I was done rewriting. It still wasn't great, but I was able to use it as a framework for future revisions.

Concentrating so hard on something freed me temporarily from the past, from my sadness. Maybe because I was writing about Tooru from an objective perspective, sometimes I even forgot him.

Just like I was absorbed in finishing my novel, Maori was absorbed in studying for university entrance exams. She still called and texted sometimes, though, and I would take a break from writing to joke around and chat like usual.

Finally, at the end of February, the contest submission deadline arrived. For the first time, I entered a piece of fiction to a writing contest.

In March, Maori learned that she'd been accepted into university. During spring break, she and I went to the park famous for its cherry blossoms to celebrate. It was the same place she, Tooru, and I had gone for a picnic during spring break of our second year of high school. This time, having almost remembered something about Tooru, she cried. She said that everything important was there inside her and that one day she would remember all of it.

I was trying to forget Tooru, and she was trying to remember him. I contemplated the contrast silently. I didn't think either of us was right or wrong. We just each had our own way of living.

In April, Maori began her first year at a different university, and I started my junior year. Although I'd already submitted my novel to the contest, I still felt it was lacking, so I continued to make revisions and even rewrote the whole thing. Sometimes, Tooru's sister got in touch. We would have a friendly cup of tea or dinner together when she was in the area.

How can I forget about Tooru?

I remembered asking her that question almost six months earlier. Compared to then, I felt a lot better. I was surprised by how helpful it was to pursue a goal. I was able to forget what I thought I would never forget. But Tooru was still there inside me. Sometimes, he appeared in my dreams. I would see someone from behind who looked like him in the halls of our high school and run desperately after him, but I could never catch up. I would wake up crying, telling myself that I had to put him in the past.

Summer came. The contest results were to be announced at the end of July in the magazine hosting it. I'd been buying the magazine every month, but I hadn't checked on the progress of the contest. Tooru's sister didn't say anything about it, either.

Now that I was a junior, I joined career center events and started studying for employment exams. The day of the contest announcement arrived before I knew it. I doubted my name would be on the list. I hadn't heard anything from the publishing company, so I knew I hadn't been selected.

I bought the magazine as usual and opened it to the page with the contest results. As I expected, my name wasn't there. I was disappointed, but there was nothing I could do about it. I wasn't good enough yet. That was fine. I would take my time and move on. As long as I kept moving forward, I should eventually arrive somewhere.

I looked through the winning entries and names.

…For a second, I thought I'd forgotten how to read Japanese.

Aside from the fiction category, there were also categories for photography and drawing. In the honorable mention column for photography was a name I knew well but could not believe was there. Next to the name of the entry…

Last Ice
Tooru Kamiya

Tooru Kamiya.

It took me a while to read and register that name. But there was no mistaking it. It really was the name I knew so well.

Like dream bleeding into reality, I was overwhelmed by an incomprehensible feeling.

What was going on? Was it just a coincidence? It must be. That was the only possibility. Tooru wasn't here anymore. I could search the whole world and never find him.

But one tiny corner of my brain felt there was a possibility, 1 percent or even less, that he was still alive.

If I die, I want you to erase me from Hino's journal.

What if everything that happened after he said that was a lie or a sham created for some reason by Tooru and his sister? What if he really was alive, and after everything calmed down, he went off to take the pictures he'd always wanted to take? What if he was living another life somewhere? A life like the character in that movie?

But that was impossible. I'd attended his wake and funeral. I'd gazed at his face as he lay in his coffin. I knew how cold it was. Or I thought I did...

Nevertheless, unable to calm my nerves, I sent his sister a text.

I saw the honorable mention winner for the photo contest. That's not Tooru, right?

After a few minutes, she replied. Whether intentionally or not, there was no clear answer in her typical warm message. Instead, she made a surprising offer.

There's going to be an award ceremony next month for the winners of the photography category, together with the literature and arts. If you like, I can put your name on the guest list for the party.

I gazed at her message, hardly breathing.

I want you to come see for yourself. It's in Tokyo. Is that all right?

Honestly, what was going on? Did she know something? If it was just a coincidence, she probably would have told me.

Thank you so much, I answered. I was full of questions, but I was still grateful she'd answered my message.

I wasn't sure if I should tell Maori, but I decided that it might just upset her pointlessly. First, I would figure out what was happening, then talk to Tooru's sister and decide what to do.

Finals ended, and my summer break began. Tooru's sister texted me about the award ceremony.

On the day of the ceremony, I have some things to do as a judge, so I can't be with you. Will you be all right?

Yes, I'll be fine, I wrote back. *Thank you for thinking to ask.*

After I sent the message, I hastily pulled up a certain picture on my phone.

There I was in my third year of high school. I was sitting in a chair in an empty classroom, smiling at the person taking the picture. It was the photo Tooru took on the day of the school festival. I had never shown it to Maori or his sister. It was taken by the Tooru that only I knew.

Would that Tooru be there at the party?

I waited uneasily for the day to come. When it did, I took the bullet train to Tokyo to make sure I got there in time for the event that evening. I'd chosen a formal outfit ahead of time. The ceremony was held in the event hall of a hotel with a long history. When I gave my name to the person at the registration desk outside the hall, I was shown in. The award ceremony with the media was taking place in a different part of the hotel, and afterward, the large crowd of attendees would head here for the party.

A steady stream of guests began pouring into the room that had been nearly empty when I arrived. When it was about to begin, the emcee took the stage and the crowd fell silent. He announced the prize winners, and they entered the hall, marking the start of the party. The winners in literature, photography, and art walked onstage. The emcee announced their names and winning entries.

Among the names was "Tooru Kamiya." I couldn't believe it. The name was familiar, but the figure dressed in a suit was not. "Tooru Kamiya" delivered his comments, and when all the winners had finished giving theirs, too, they walked down from the stage. Then it was time for casual mingling, and the winners were surrounded by people wanting to talk to them.

I walked forward silently. My throat was scratchy and dry. From a slight distance, I gazed at "Tooru Kamiya" in his suit, burning the image into my mind. He noticed my eyes on him and glanced at me. He was shocked. For a few seconds, we stared at each other. I felt like we had looked at each other like this before. When was it? Where? I, too, was overcome by surprise. He smiled and walked over to me.

"Wataya."

It wasn't the real Tooru Kamiya. It was my fellow university classmate Tooru Naruse, who had accepted the prize in Tooru Kamiya's name.

Last Ice

1

Until now, my life has been uneventful. I never felt strongly driven to start or end anything. Fittingly for someone named Tooru, which means "transparent," I lived a quiet life, like an invisible man. What else could I do? I had nothing to offer. No talent, no personality…

But was that enough?

One day, I suddenly began to wonder. The spark was my breakup with Wataya. I'd known from the start that she was out of my league, and more importantly, I hadn't held up my end of the deal.

I'll date you, but under one condition. Don't fall in love with me. Can you promise me that?

I knew I was holding on to a relationship that was over, but after we broke up, I thought a lot about what I should have said when she asked me that.

I don't like nice guys.

Should I have given up when she drew that line right at the start? At first, I took her words at face value. I thought she simply disliked nice people. But when I talked to her best friend, Maori Hino, I realized I might have been wrong—that the person she couldn't forget had been kind.

I think my personality might have been slightly similar to his. Or maybe an inferior version. I was somewhat nice, somewhat honest, somewhat clever, kind of…

For the first time in my life, I felt ashamed of having nothing to offer.

If I wasn't just an inferior version, if I had some special quality or ability, would Wataya have stayed with me? If I obtained that sort of distinction, would she consider coming back to me?

A literary magazine happened to lie nearby. The magazine was currently holding a writing contest judged by Keiko Nishikawa, the author Wataya admired. I'd sought out a copy after talking with Hino at the family restaurant. I'd realized that Wataya might be thinking of entering the contest, since she was writing a novel. I knew it was pointless to buy the magazine for that reason, of course. All I could do was watch her attempt from a distance.

I'd assumed the contest was only for literature, but it turned out there were categories for photography and art, too. My eyes rested on the word *photography* for a long time. I never thought I'd return to photography in this way.

You don't have what it takes to really throw yourself into something, Naruse. You're just a dabbler with a few tricks up your sleeve…

Every time I saw that word, *photography*, something inside me ached. In elementary school, I had an innocent love for taking pictures. I'd first gotten interested on a school trip to a tourist spot. There was a group of girls in my class who wanted someone to take pictures of them. They were so happy when I volunteered. But that wasn't all. When I pointed the camera at them and took their photo, they all smiled. When other groups of kids saw me taking their picture, they asked me to take theirs, too. The same thing happened. I pointed the camera; they smiled. I'd never taken pictures before, so this came as a surprise.

I learned that photographs could make people smile.

After that, I volunteered to take pictures at every school event. As I walked around the sports festival or school festival with my camera, everyone would gather around me, begging me to take their picture. I graduated from elementary school, and luckily enough, the junior high I went to had a photography club. Everyone in the club was great, and when there was a school event, the school advisers and student council always asked us to take lots of pictures. Photos of smiling people.

These photos are just records of events.

There was this one strange guy in the club, a third-year named Sakurai. For better or worse, everyone else in the club was there for social reasons. Sakurai was the only one who was serious about photography. He hated the club because of this, but he stayed for the free access to equipment. He made the other members uncomfortable.

But he was an incredible photographer. I heard he'd won prizes for his photos starting in elementary school, and by junior high, his photos were better than what most adults could shoot. He raked in top prizes from famous photography contests. I truly respected him. He was cynical, but even that seemed cool to me. I kept talking to him no matter how mean he was to me, and maybe it's conceited of me to think this, but I don't think he disliked me. When I showed him pictures I'd taken, he would smile, despite the fact I could tell he was disappointed with my work.

"Naruse, why do you take pictures?" he asked me one day before summer break. The other club members were out taking photos, and we were alone in the club room.

"Because when I take them, everyone smiles."

"…I'm not surprised to hear that coming from you," he said, smirking at me like I was a child, like he always did.

"What about you?" I asked.

"Me? …Because photos make me special."

That hadn't occurred to me. To me, pictures were linked to smiling people. They didn't change me. Sakurai smirked at my reaction.

"Listen, Naruse. The photos everyone in this club takes, including yours, are just records of events. You don't frame what's there with any intention. You're not making pictures."

"Photos can be made?"

He smirked again at my idiotic question.

"I'll teach you how to make photos, if you're interested."

Maybe it was a whim of his, but the summer of my first year of junior high, Sakurai taught me how to take—or rather, make—photographs. He drilled the basic but crucial techniques into me. The outcome was that I won a prize in a photo contest for junior high school students at the end of summer vacation. The prize was just one of dozens of honorable mentions, but to me it was a huge achievement. My family, classmates, and fellow club members were as happy as I was.

I thought Sakurai would be happy, too. I'd told him I was entering the contest, and he'd said I should take and choose the picture by myself. When the two of us happened to be alone in the club room, I showed him the photo and told him I'd won honorable mention. He gave the picture a hard look, and then for some reason, he had on a sad expression.

"Are you happy with honorable mention?"

His voice sounded horribly loud and cold in the empty room.

"Happy with it? I'm more than happy. It's a good memory."

"You don't want to try for a bigger award?"

He was looking at me the way he looked at things he was photographing. That is, very closely. I examined my feelings before answering.

"I hardly feel like I deserve honorable mention. It's probably rude to say this to the person who taught me, but I think it was a fluke…"

"If you really made an effort, I think the outcome would have been different."

"What?"

"I taught you how to make photographs at least good enough to have won first prize in that contest. You have talent. If you didn't, I wouldn't have taught you. But you decided what your own limit was and confined yourself to it."

I thought he was angry. He wasn't. He was sad. Maybe he'd been searching for someone like himself, someone who took photography seriously. But I betrayed him. I left him alone.

"You don't have what it takes to really throw yourself into something, Naruse. You're just a dabbler with a few tricks up your sleeve…"

He walked out of the room, leaving me with those words.

Sakurai had left quietly, but his impact on my life was powerful. Both of us stayed in Photography Club, and we saw each other now and then. However, I felt weirdly nervous around him, and after that day, I never talked to him again. Before long, he graduated. Then when my graduation approached, I heard that instead of going to high school, he'd become an apprentice with a professional photographer in Tokyo.

Three years later, around the time of my high school graduation, the members of our junior high photography club got together. One of them was an older student who attended the university I was about to enter, and who I would later see often. But Sakurai didn't come. He was only two years older than me, but I heard he was already working independently as a photographer. Everyone was praising the pictures he posted on social media. I pulled them up on my own phone.

Photos aren't taken; they're made.

In an era when anyone can take a pretty picture on their phone, Sakurai was forging his own, unique way of making photographs. They were beautiful, and many people admired them. If I was a mass product, he was thoroughly his own person with something unique to offer. I thought about my current reality.

You don't have what it takes to really throw yourself into some-thing, Naruse. You're just a dabbler with a few tricks up your sleeve…

His words still pierced my heart. I wasn't a special person. I wasn't a person who could take anything seriously.

Every time I heard or saw the word *photograph*, Sakurai's words echoed in my mind. I looked the other way and accepted my disappointing self. I gave up on myself… It was only natural that a person like me wouldn't be able to draw the interest of the person they loved.

I gripped the literary magazine. I stared at it intently. If I acquired some special ability or quality, would Wataya be surprised? Would she recognize my value and become interested in me?

I wanted that. I wanted it now, desperately.

For the first time, I—an ordinary person of average ability who had always allowed the currents of life to carry me along—desired something. I yearned for it.

After that day, I decided I would take off running. All I needed was resolve. I told myself I didn't need anything else. In retrospect, maybe that's what it means to throw yourself into something.

I met Sakurai two days later, in the middle of summer break. I wanted to study photography with him again. I *had* to. If I was going to change, I had to go back to that point in my life.

I tracked him down on social media. It seemed a friend of his was having a show in Tokyo, where he worked, and he was helping out. I got up the courage to visit. Some people were there for the show, while others who seemed involved with running it were talking quietly together in a group. I recognized Sakurai immediately. I walked over to him. He looked up at me. At first, he was suspicious of me, but then I saw recognition dawn on his face.

"I hate honorable mentions."

Time seemed to freeze. He widened his eyes.

But time hadn't really stopped. It had moved forward. And it still was. It marched forward mercilessly whether I did anything or not.

"It's taken me six years to say that. But I finally did it. I'm not satisfied with honorable mentions anymore. There's something I want no matter what. So…"

Sakurai's friends and the other people in the gallery were staring at me. It was a supremely embarrassing situation. I had shown up out of nowhere and was talking nonsense. But I didn't care. I didn't care if I was shameless. The only thing I cared about was not being apathetic.

"Please teach me how to make photographs again."

Suddenly, he grinned. I'd seen that smile a few times during the summer he taught me photography. And I hadn't seen it since.

"Naruse, I swear... You show up after all these years and ask me that?"

In spite of his words, he seemed happy.

"Seems like you turned into quite an interesting person," he said, with a hint of kindness. There were things I wanted to talk to him about, but we didn't need to do that right then. Still smiling, he continued on. "I'm down. I was just looking for an assistant I could use for free. You ready for that?"

In exchange for him teaching me photography, I was to work for free as his assistant. I didn't argue, and we decided on the length of my apprenticeship then and there. I suggested one year, as the results of the contest I wanted to win would be announced in about a year. He agreed.

At that stage, I still could have backed out. I could have apologized to Sakurai, slunk back to my studio apartment, and returned to being my old self without having changed a thing. But I'd gone there because I didn't like the old me. It didn't matter if the whole year came to nothing. It was no different from taking a gap year between high school and college. Even so, I didn't want to be a burden on my parents. After I left the show, I called them to ask about taking a year off school. I knew that if I submitted the paperwork before the second semester began, I wouldn't have to pay tuition. I could also end the lease on my studio. When I started school again, I could commute to campus from my parents' house if I left early enough. The studio apartment was a kind of present from them, and it had been a luxury from the start.

It was Saturday, so my dad was home. He was surprised when I said I wanted to take time off school. Naturally, he asked why.

"There's something I want to do right now no matter what," I answered.

"Do you have to do it right now? Would it be too hard to keep going to school while you're doing it?"

"Yes. If I don't follow through with this, I think I'll regret it. The thing I need to do right now is even more urgent than when I had to study for the university entrance exams in high school. I also see it as testing myself in a way."

My father hesitated. I had never asked for anything like this in the past, and now I was blindsiding him with this sudden, vague request.

"…How long do you plan to take off?"

"A year. If I submit the forms now, there won't be any fees, and I'll be able to end the lease on my apartment, too. When I go back to school, I'll commute from home. So you won't have to pay for an apartment or lose anything financially."

I told him I wanted to study photography. I also told him about Sakurai and the contest I wanted to enter. After a long pause, my father said, "All right. But I don't want your mother to worry, so I'd like you to contact us once a month."

I thanked him, reflexively bowing there on the street. After that, I went through with it, taking a year off school to apprentice with Sakurai.

The deadline for the contest was February of the following year. I intended to work like a madman during the intervening six months. If I didn't see any results by then, however, I planned to stop by that point. There might be other ways to go about it, and there might be a way forward even if I failed, but I put that out of my mind for the time being. I was going to push myself to the limit and win the heart of the person I loved.

That day, after talking to Sakurai, I went back to my apartment near campus. I felt a bit guilty, but I asked my parents to handle the paperwork for breaking the lease while I packed my things, sending my books back home and my clothes and other essentials to Sakurai's apartment in Tokyo. The rest I threw away.

Sakurai's place was on the older side, with one bedroom and a living room, and bare concrete walls. He used it as his studio as well as his living space.

"Well, Naruse, here we go," he said when I moved in.

"I'm looking forward to it," I answered.

He'd agreed to provide basic room and board. I slept on the sofa in the studio, which wasn't the best for my back, but I settled in. As his assistant, most of my work involved physical labor. I lugged his equipment to studios and outdoor locations and arranged his photo shoots. In between, I learned photography from him.

Idiotically, I hadn't brought my own camera when I went to apprentice with him. Instead of getting mad, he laughed and lent me an SLR camera he wasn't using anymore. I told him about the prize I desperately wanted to win, and the reason. He cracked up laughing.

"Man, Naruse, you really did turn into an interesting guy when I wasn't looking."

As a professional photographer, he was focused on increasing the value of his product. He photographed both objects and people. He approached every job enthusiastically, and he created shockingly beautiful pictures. Sometimes, with his permission, I photographed the same subject as him. But I never managed to take the kind of pictures he achieved. It wasn't a matter of different cameras; it was the skill of the people using them.

"Your pictures are too conventional, Naruse," he told me one day as he drove us to a shoot. "You didn't come here to become conventional, did you? Get a little stupid, okay? Break your own rules. Then you'll realize just how commonplace and small those rules are, just how impractical and inappropriate and boring."

I lugged equipment, set up shoots, looked through the finder, and pressed the shutter. He also taught me current digital photography techniques. A day never passed without me picking up the camera. I also cleaned, did laundry, ironed, and cooked. Sakurai said I could skip the ironing, but as I'd made a resolution, I always at least ironed the handkerchiefs. Before I knew it, fall had arrived. There are no vacations in this field, and we left early in the morning and got back late at night.

When winter began, something surprising happened. Wataya texted me.

I heard you're taking time off school.

I was busy as always that day, so I didn't notice her message. I only saw it that night when the day was winding down. Holding back my excitement, I wrote back.

Good to hear from you, Wataya. Thank you for your message. I'm…taking time off for some personal reasons.

Ah. Are you doing okay?

Yes, I'm fine. Things are tough, but I'm getting by.

What are you doing these days?

Working all the time.

After I decided to take a year off, I got in touch with my university friends. Since it would have been complicated to explain everything, I told them I had some personal stuff going on. And I'd just told Wataya I was working. I wondered if she'd heard about me and gotten in touch because she was worried. Or maybe, given how kind she was, she worried that our breakup was the reason I was taking time off and texted me because she felt bad.

Uh, Wataya? I wrote, thinking that might be the case. *I'm really happy that we're talking again.*

Then I sent another message to let her know I appreciated her.

I'm so glad I met you.

But everything I did to you was horrible, she replied.

I was the one who'd fallen for her when she clearly had no interest in me, followed her around, and broken her condition for dating. She hadn't done anything horrible.

That's not true. You were out of my league from the start.

I'd always known that. After all…

I don't have anything to offer.

Right after sending that message, I started worrying that I'd made things too heavy. I changed the subject.

How about you? How are you doing?

Me? Same as always. Going to class, helping my mom with work sometimes.

I felt relieved that I'd managed to change the subject, but her next message caught me off guard.

Also, I'm writing a novel.

Really, a novel?

Yeah. I'm thinking of submitting it to a contest. Don't tell anyone, okay?

…It seemed like I'd guessed right. Although the judges and division were different for literature and photography, she was probably planning to enter the same contest as me. Which meant that if I entered under my own name, she might notice.

I only had a few more minutes left until my break ended, so I said goodbye and signed off. Before she contacted me, part of me had felt it would be enough just to make the final round and have my work printed in the magazine. That would be an achievement in its own right. But that was just my pride talking. I was only trying to prevent myself from getting hurt if I went all-out for what I wanted but didn't get it. That wasn't the right attitude. It wouldn't get me anywhere.

I made up my mind to achieve my goal. If I couldn't, then I'd take the pain.

The first time I noticed a clear change in the way I was taking pictures was around mid-December. People have all sorts of opinions and ideas, but I understood deep down that photography was a creative act. You didn't take pictures; you made them. You created them with the same intention involved in other forms of art.

Sometimes Sakurai invited me to walk around the city in December with our cameras. We took pictures of all kinds of things. From landscapes to objects. Cats in back alleys and birds taking flight. People going about their lives. Smiles.

When I first came to Tokyo and started taking pictures again, there would occasionally, just by chance, be one picture that stood out among the rest. I went about changing chance into inevitability.

I wasn't a natural like Sakurai, but it was unbelievably fun. Making photos not as a record of events but as creative works.

"Think you're ready to start taking pictures for the contest soon?"

Photographers never rest. There was work on New Year's Eve and New Year's Day. When that calmed down, around the middle of January, Sakurai brought up the contest. The deadline was a month and a half away. By that time, I was completely used to life as a photographer's assistant. My back didn't even hurt from sleeping on the sofa anymore.

"Have you decided on your subject?"

"I have. I'm thinking of using a spring."

"A spring? Oh, man. A simple subject like that without any spatial expansiveness is really hard to shoot. I'm not saying impressing the judges is everything, but if you want a prize, you better choose something a little grander."

"...I see your point. But I really have my heart set on this. The woman I'm in love with, her first name means 'spring,'" I admitted bashfully.

He burst out laughing. He told me in that case to go right ahead and promised to give me plenty of advice. He asked what my plan was. I already had an image of the photograph I wanted to take. I'd figured out where I could take it, too. There are quite a few parks in Tokyo, and one of them had a natural spring. The park didn't have an entry fee, and I'd confirmed that photography was allowed.

A cold, frozen spring.

I wanted to capture the moment when sunlight shone on it, and the ice cracked.

When I asked Sakurai, he said it wasn't ideal but nevertheless gave his approval. However, he warned that the shooting conditions would be tough.

Ice only forms below zero degrees Celsius. Every night before I went to bed, I checked the weather forecast for the next morning's temperatures. When the conditions were right, I woke up before dawn, when the sky was tinted ultramarine, and set out alone to take pictures.

My breath was white in the cold air, and the streets were so quiet, it felt like there wasn't a soul in all of Tokyo.

The first time I saw ice over the spring, I was deeply moved. I waited there in the cold for the first light. I gazed through the viewfinder, waiting for the moment when the ice cracked.

The frozen spring was richly nuanced. It glittered transiently, reflecting the sun. Warming my hands so they wouldn't become numb, I waited for the ice to crack. At long last, the moment arrived, and the click of the shutter sounded like a pebble being thrown into the spring. I checked the picture, but I knew it was impossible to have gotten it on the first try. The composition was wrong, the lighting was off, and all in all, it was nowhere near what I'd envisioned.

I reworked the image in my mind, returning again and again to shoot the same moment. I showed the pictures to Sakurai, but he just shook his head. January passed without any success. Then the first week of February passed, and the second. As the deadline steadily approached, I quietly began to panic.

It was around that time when I first heard of Tooru Kamiya.

From time to time, Hino and I exchanged texts. In December and January, she seemed especially busy studying for the university entrance exams. One day in February, she said she'd finished all the tests she planned to take. We were texting about that when she brought up Wataya.

By the way, I wanted to tell you something related to Izumi.

I hadn't told Hino I was taking time off school, but I'd let her know that Wataya had contacted me in winter. I'm sure she was busy studying, but she still sent me a warm message saying *I'm glad you two talked again.* After that, whenever she met up with Wataya or talked to her on the phone, she would text me letting me know. But this time was different.

I was waiting to talk about it until I finished my exams...and since they're over, I want to tell you. In high school, there was a guy named Tooru Kamiya. He was my boyfriend and Izumi's friend. Maybe she told you about him?

Tooru Kamiya. I'd never heard the name before, so I was slightly surprised.

No, it's news to me. So you did have a high school boyfriend?

She'd told me before that she'd never dated anyone. It stuck in my mind because I thought it was rather surprising, but I asked because I thought maybe I remembered wrong. She didn't reply right away. After a short pause, her response arrived.

It's kind of complicated. Do you mind if I call you? You know Izumi and me, so I'd like to take this chance to tell you about it.

I agreed somewhat warily, and she called me through the messaging app. That was when I learned about her unusual high school years. She told me she'd had anterograde amnesia and that she had a boyfriend during that time. He died right after they graduated from high school...and according to his last wish, Wataya had erased all mention of him from Hino's journals.

Now that her exams were done, Hino said she was trying to remember her boyfriend. She didn't care if it was just small things; she wanted to know who this person, Tooru Kamiya, had been. I listened very quietly as she talked about it. I was surprised to learn about her difficult past but even more shaken by something else.

Why don't you like nice guys?

Nice people are good people. That kind of person…dies young.

The words that Wataya had said were falling into place.

I…don't like nice guys.

It was him. Tooru Kamiya. He was the person she couldn't forget.

The person she had fallen in love with was her best friend's boyfriend…and he was dead. Fulfilling his last wish, she had erased his existence from Hino's mind. But even if Hino forgot him, Wataya couldn't.

There's something I can't forget…though I know I need to forget it. Maybe I thought that if I had a pretend relationship, all of that would go away. If we kept things on a surface level and just had fun.

The truth was, she was suffering. I hadn't understood her at all.

"Um…are you okay, Naruse? What's wrong?"

Hino's voice brought me back to the present. I considered telling her what I'd just realized, but because of her amnesia, she might not know about Wataya's feelings. I didn't want to carelessly tell her something like that.

"I'm just surprised. Thank you for telling me."

"There's hardly anyone I can tell. Just having you listen helps me make sense of it. Sorry this turned into such a long conversation. But thank you."

We talked a little more and then hung up. I was alone at night in the studio. When I walked over to the window, I saw my own reflection like I had that time at the restaurant.

Tooru Kamiya. That was the person Wataya loved. Had loved.

He had the same name as me.

I thought back to what Hino and I had figured out about the person Wataya might have liked in high school. He was kind, good at housework, thoughtful toward his family, and serious. That probably described Tooru Kamiya. I was a mere inferior version of him. I probably wasn't even close. But there was one thing he couldn't beat me at. I knew he couldn't have loved Wataya more than I did. That alone was where I didn't lose in comparison. I couldn't lose.

I realized something then. The "special thing" I was after—maybe I didn't really need it. Maybe I just wanted an opportunity. An opportunity to tell her how I felt again...

I thought about that on my way to the park to photograph the spring. Even early in the morning in February, it wasn't always below zero. I only had a few chances to get the shot I wanted. Fortunately, that morning, the spring was frozen over. The sky wasn't cloudy, either. The air in the park was still and clear, and the only movement was the white breath I exhaled.

Eventually, a ray of sunlight shone on the park. It reached the spring. As I gazed at it through the viewfinder, I thought of the face of the woman I loved. During the time I waited in silence, I wondered why I loved her. Was it because she had a nice figure? Because she was beautiful?

Neither was the deciding factor. Plenty of women had nice bodies. I met them and talked to them at photo shoots. But I only ever felt strongly drawn to Wataya. To that sad, lonely expression of hers...

Naruse, why do you take pictures?

Because when I take pictures, everyone smiles.

Maybe because I was holding a camera, the past whispered to me, and I widened my eyes reflexively. I was an ordinary person of average ability, and I had let life carry me along. But I still had something I valued. Why had I forgotten? I had brought it around with me in elementary school, taking great care to protect it. Had I left it somewhere, along with my camera?

I loved to see people smile. When I pointed the camera at them and took their picture, everyone would smile. That was why I liked photography.

I wanted Wataya to smile. From the bottom of my heart, I wanted to make her grin. I didn't know what she had gone through in the past. Did that matter? Could I still reach her?

Just then, something in my field of vision moved. I heard the ice crack. I pressed the shutter with a wish in mind.

Last Ice

That was the name Sakurai and I thought up for the shot I took that morning. It meant the last freeze of the year before spring. Technically, the last frost date of the year in Tokyo usually happens in late March, but Sakurai said that wasn't important when creating a work of art.

"This is your photograph and no one else's. You don't need to stick to facts or common sense for any part of it," he said.

I entered that shot in the contest. I'd been away from school for almost half a year. I had thrown myself completely into photography, placing it at the center of my life. Maybe to Sakurai it was still considered poor work, but I'd created a photograph I was satisfied with.

All that remained was to fill out the necessary paperwork and send it in. There was a line for both my real name and an artist's pseudonym, but I intended to use my real name. I wanted Wataya, who I expected to enter the literature division, to realize it was me.

Last Ice, Tooru Naruse.

But then a thought crossed my mind. I considered it, examining my feelings. A photograph was made, not taken. What had I wanted to express through that work of art? I think a part of me subconsciously knew the answer. From the bottom of my heart, I wanted to make Wataya smile. I wanted to erase the frozen expression from her face.

…But maybe I wasn't the one to do that.

Suddenly, my own name struck me as an obstacle. I shouldn't be there. So I decided to change it. It felt as if it was meant to happen, photo and artist name included.

Last Ice, Tooru Kamiya.

Tooru Kamiya, the person Wataya loved. What was he like? How did he smile?

Maybe my decision was wrong. But I didn't intend to profane the dead or pointlessly upset Wataya. Using Tooru Kamiya's name was the final step in creating this work of art, imbuing it with respect for the person she loved. In that way, I finished my contest entry.

Finally, spring arrived. Spring is a busy season for photographers. While I was working on the contest entry, Sakurai had given me a break from helping him with his job. To pay him back for the favor, I worked especially hard as his assistant that season.

A few months later, to my surprise, I received a phone call telling me my photo had been selected for an award. After asking for detailed information about my idea behind creating the piece, they told me which award it was. Honorable mention. One of five. When I got off the phone, I didn't know what to think. I'd reached my goal. I hadn't wasted all this time. But…

"So, what's the news?"

When I walked back into the studio, Sakurai was grinning, having guessed what was going on from the way I'd rushed out of the room with my phone. I felt like crying when I saw his smile. I was happy but, at the same time, ashamed. I'd poured everything I had into that picture, but I'd still failed to live up to his expectations.

"I got…an honorable mention," I told him. The room went silent. Okay, it was silent to start with. But my own heart stood still. I couldn't bring myself to look at his face.

After a moment, he walked over to me. I'd disappointed him. I'd made him sad. I thought he would walk past me, fed up, never wanting to see a loser like me again. I thought I'd never see his warm smile again.

"You did good, Naruse."

But his response was different. He recognized what I'd done. He thumped me on the shoulder. When I looked up, he was smiling.

"But I got an honorable mention again…"

"Naruse. You put your heart into it, didn't you? Twenty-four hours a day, you thought about photography, carried your camera around, looked through the viewfinder until your eyes hurt. You lost yourself in making pictures."

"Twenty-four hours...might be an overstatement. I did sleep."

He smiled at my idiotic answer. I smiled back.

"But you're right—when I was awake, I was usually thinking about photography."

"Yeah? And how was it? Do you like photography?"

"I love it."

That was one thing I could say with confidence. And I looked him in the eye when I did. Still smiling, he looked down and said a bit shyly, "Naruse, do you remember when you asked me why I take pictures?"

"It was before summer vacation in my first year of junior high. I remember it well."

"So do I. My answer was that photography makes me a special person. But I liked your answer, too."

He smiled as he asked his next question.

"So tell me, Naruse. Why do you take pictures?"

I already knew the answer.

"Because when I take pictures, everyone smiles," I said, repeating my answer from back then.

An exceptionally bright smile spread across his face. A warm smile. I think that's what his true self must have looked like when we were kids.

I received an email from the publishing company informing me that the award ceremony would take place in Tokyo in August. Although Sakurai said not to worry about it, I worked with him up until the day before the ceremony, while getting ready to go back to school at the same time. I planned to move back home, as I wanted to tell my parents about the prize in person. I was going to contact Hino, too, but not say anything to my university friends, because that would be embarrassing.

Wataya was the exception. I planned to go see her, with my photograph and award as my support. I was going to tell her my feelings again—tell her I liked her. I wanted her to know about my feelings once again.

On the day of the award ceremony, I stood in front of Sakurai's apartment dressed in the suit I'd bought for my university entrance ceremony and said my goodbyes to him. Just before I left, he placed the camera of his that I'd been using for the past year around my neck and said, "This is yours now. You've become a first-rate cameraman."

We both smiled. He had work to do, so we parted ways there.

"Whether she says yes or no, bring that woman you're in love with over here sometime," he said.

"I think that would be hard if she was to reject me."

"Shut up."

He smiled right to the end.

"Bye," he said, raising one hand. I bowed and quietly turned away.

"You don't have to do it for a job," he said. I looked back at him. "But keep taking pictures."

"Thank you for everything. I hope we meet again one day."

I headed toward the subway station, looking up to keep myself from crying.

I was able to stay calmer than I'd expected at the award ceremony. For once, I was on the other side of the camera, having my picture taken. I tried to smile as brightly as I could and got scolded for it. Everyone laughed. Afterward, at the party, a lot of people called out to me. I was surprised by how many people had seen my picture.

But something else surprised me even more. As I was talking to everyone, I sensed someone's eyes on me and turned around. A beautiful woman wearing a muted-colored dress was looking at me. I stared at her because she looked like someone I knew. No—she didn't just look like her. It was her. Wataya. She was standing right there. She must have realized that I was "Tooru Kamiya," because she was staring at me in surprise.

2

"Hey, Wataya! I went to high school with this here freshman. He says he likes you."

More than a year had passed since a guy in my class said that to me at a drinking party. I only attended as it would have been rude to turn down their invitation. I looked in the direction he was pointing and saw a flustered guy. He looked naive, like the brand-new freshman he was. I vaguely remembered seeing him somewhere, but I couldn't remember exactly where.

"Really? Is that true?" I asked.

"Um, well, it's just…"

It was my second year of university, and I still couldn't forget Tooru.

If this guy was going to fall for someone, he should fall for someone else. For his own sake.

"You should forget about me. I'm a real pain in the ass," I said, intentionally putting him in an awkward spot. But my attempt failed in the face of his honesty. He answered, undiscouraged.

"I doubt that's true! You're a wonderful person."

It surprised me.

"You don't know anything yet," our mutual friend said, teasing him. Everyone laughed.

"But it's like I can just tell, just from being around her…"

I thought, *He's an odd one.* And he slightly piqued my interest. A little later, he was prodded to come sit by me. I didn't know what to call him, so I asked him his name.

"So what's your name?"

"Uh, Naruse. Tooru Naruse."

We were drinking at a pub near the university. Another group of rowdy students was nearby. But in that moment, the world went silent for me.

When the noise filled my ears again, I asked him another question.

"…Tooru? What character do you write it with?"

"The one for 'clear.' Maybe my name is accurate—I don't have much of a personality."

Less than two months later, this Tooru Naruse told me he liked me. I agreed to date him because I wanted to forget the other Tooru. I learned various things about him while we were dating. He looked smart but was slightly unreliable. His personality seemed kind of weak. I couldn't imagine him setting out to achieve something of his own free will and grabbing it for himself.

But now he had won an award under the name Tooru Kamiya. Despite his humble demeanor, he was standing tall in the reception hall.

He walked toward me.

"It's been a while. I'm happy to see you again. I didn't have time to think about the possibility that you might be here, so you caught me off guard."

True to his words, he looked shocked. I was, too. There was so much I didn't know. Why was he here? He'd told me he disliked taking pictures and being photographed. Then why had he entered the photo contest?

And why under the name Tooru Kamiya?

Compared to a year ago, he seemed to have a backbone that held him up as he stood there. He asked me hesitantly, "After the party, do you have time to talk? I wanted to meet with you after I got back home, but…if you have time today, there are some things I'd like to tell you."

"All right," I answered. "I have some questions myself… I'll be waiting for you."

We decided where to meet afterward. There were heaps of things I wanted to ask him, but someone from the prize committee came, and Naruse had left with them, saying we'd meet later. I watched him walk away. Within the short time we'd known each other, I had seen that back many times. Yes—something had changed in the past year. He wasn't the same simply kind Naruse that I knew.

"Izumi," a familiar voice said. It was Tooru's sister. She must have known Naruse because she smiled when she saw me gazing after him.

"Did…you two talk?"

"Yes, a little… He goes to my university."

"So I've heard. I was quite surprised when I saw my brother's name in the list of finalists for the photography contest."

I could only imagine. Especially because she knew that Tooru had been interested in photography.

"When I saw his age and university, I realized he was a year behind you at the same school. His real name was different. After the final decisions were made, I asked the person in charge of the photography division to find out more about him for me…and I learned why he'd used the name Tooru Kamiya."

She paused, then said, "Please don't scold him for it."

I wasn't sure what she meant, but just then someone called for her. We'd arranged to meet the next day, so I watched quietly as her slender figure receded.

In the past and even in the present, all kinds of things happened without my knowing.

Less than an hour later, the party ended. I walked over to the hotel lounge. Shortly after, Naruse texted me, and a few minutes after that, he showed up in that suit I still wasn't used to seeing him in. We sat down across from each other for the first time in a long while.

"All of this has been so unexpected," I said. There were so many things I needed to say, so many questions I wanted to ask, but that was the first thing that came out of my mouth.

"It's the same for me. I never imagined I would see you here."

Maybe it would have been better to meet as fellow prizewinners. But I hadn't made the cut. He, on the other hand, had poured himself so completely into photography that he was able to win a prize.

"So you're a photographer. Since when?"

"Strictly speaking, since elementary school. But I was just a shutter-happy kid back then. I started paying more attention to what I was doing in the summer of junior high. I found a kind of mentor."

He told me about his experiences related to photography in junior high. How he met his mentor, then they went their different ways. How he had reconnected with the same guy a year ago and taken up photography again.

"But why did you decide to enter the contest? You'd given up photography before that, right?"

I still had questions even after hearing his story. He gazed at me. Finally, he answered. Without flustering, and with earnest eyes.

"Because I like you."

He had confessed to me once before, but the words had a different ring this time. Infinitely calm, and even serene.

"Really…? You quit university because of me?"

"I felt like if I didn't change then, I never would. It made sense that you weren't interested in me, because I wasn't able to do anything with my whole heart. I wanted to try. And…I wanted to meet you again once I could feel proud of myself. The contest was an opportunity. I wanted to tell you how I felt one more time."

I was on the verge of being moved. His time, all of his effort, had been directed at me. He liked me. He wanted to catch my eye. He'd gone as far as quitting school and roaming around Tokyo taking pictures for my sake…

"That's going kind of far, isn't it?" I mumbled, furrowing my brow. He smiled shyly.

"I think I wanted to go that far. There are some people who want their feelings to be reciprocated so badly, they're willing to go that far for them. Not many things in life can make you that happy."

His words overlapped with the other Tooru's words in my mind. Those words I should have been forgetting came bubbling up inside me.

If there's something I can do with a little extra effort or something I want to do, then I feel happy to do it.

Relationships always changed things when I wasn't looking. That's what happened with Tooru. I thought he was a cold fish, but his relationship with Maori warmed him up through and through. It was the same with Naruse. I thought he was a younger guy with no distinguishing characteristics, and now look at him. I was walled off from all of that, but I watched it change other people from close up. I was the only one who never changed, and before I knew it...

"You...liked Tooru Kamiya, didn't you?"

I looked up at his words. I asked how he knew who Tooru was, and he told me. He also told me why he decided to enter his photograph under Tooru's name. Many things he said surprised me, but I wasn't mad at him. Only Tooru's sister and I knew that he had been interested in photography, so to everyone else, it probably seemed like a coincidence.

"When Kamiya was alive...he told me that one day he wanted to become a photographer, so I was even more surprised to see his name."

"Kamiya, really?"

"Yes. I know it's impossible, but I wondered if he was somehow still alive... Once in high school, he took a picture of me. It was a great picture."

Overwhelmed by sentimentality, I told him what I'd never told any-one else. I thought of the photo on my phone.

"What was it like?"

"Just an ordinary picture he took on my phone."

"Would you show it to me?"

"I'm sorry."

It wasn't something I could show another person. And to a photog-rapher, it might not be as great as I said.

"I really want to see it. A picture that Tooru Kamiya took of you…"

But I gave in to his eagerness. Maybe, behind my embarrassment, I had wanted all along to show someone that photo he left behind. I took out my phone and pulled up the picture, then handed it to Naruse. He gazed at it silently. He was completely still.

"Thank you," he said, handing my phone back to me. For some rea-son, his eyes were glistening with tears.

"Why are you crying?" I asked. He wiped his eyes, flustered. Finally, he answered, choosing his words slowly.

"Because…I can see how much you cared about him. Also, because what I wish for is right there in that picture."

"What you wish for?"

"I wanted to make you smile. You acted bright and cheerful at uni-versity, but were you ever truly happy?"

"I…"

"I wanted to make you happy. I think that's why I fell for you. Because I hoped you would smile…like the way you do in that photo."

Make me smile.

The thoughts and feelings I had on the day Tooru took that picture came flooding back. I remembered how we'd walked around the school festival together, how I'd smiled so much, my cheeks hurt. I remembered Tooru Kamiya, the person I liked so much, so close to me, our shoulders could have touched. I couldn't help smiling around him. I forgot my sadness and worries and just grinned and felt secure. I really did like him.

"When did you start liking him?" Naruse asked.

"…I don't know. It happened without my realizing it, and I gave up without realizing it, too. By my third year of high school, I was already…"

I glanced down and happened to see my phone. There I was smiling back at myself. I missed that smile. I'd forgotten it completely.

"What did you like about him?"

I fell silent.

"How revolting he was."

Naruse looked surprised, but he nevertheless smiled tenderly. The memories kept flooding back.

"I thought he was a cold person, like me…but he warmed up to Maori. He said he wanted to make the Maori of every day smile. He wasn't even embarrassed to say that… He was kind, so kind, it was revolting. He was good at housework and made a better cup of black tea than I could. He never thought about what he'd gain out of a situation. And, and…"

Tears were starting to blur my vision. He'd meant so much to me. I closed my eyes, and all I saw was his smile. But he wasn't looking at me. That smile wasn't for me. I didn't care. Their happiness, Maori's and Tooru's, was my own happiness. I wanted them to be happy forever. To always be smiling at each other. But he died suddenly, despite everything. He was kind, and the gods took him from us. They left behind the bad ones like me and took the endlessly kind Tooru. Even though if he had lived, he would have made so many people happy, especially Maori.

After all, she recovered from amnesia. They would have become an ordinary couple. Smiling, always smiling. Then one day, they would have gotten married and had children, created their own ordinary family... The past would have become something to laugh about. Their children, who would have known nothing of their painful past, wouldn't have believed the story when they heard it. But I, the best friend, would have told them it was all true. Maybe sometimes my chest would ache with pain. But I still would have celebrated their happiness with all my heart. That was the life they should have lived...

After I had haltingly laid bare my feelings, I covered my face with my hands. I knew crying wouldn't change anything. Life gave and took away according to its own whims. My loving parents, my first crush, even human life. Tears couldn't bring any of that back. But because I was so helpless, I could only cry.

I looked down, crying quietly. Then, something was held out to me. I lowered my shaking hands from my face. I couldn't believe it. I felt like I had seen the same thing once before...this brilliant white object. A neatly ironed handkerchief. Just like the one Tooru, who cared so much about being sanitary, used to carry with him...

"Could I ever take his place?"

With lowered eyebrows, he smiled at me as I took the handkerchief. He was always kind. I went out with him because I wanted to forget the other Tooru. But I never called him by his first name. In my heart, Tooru would always be Tooru Kamiya. I felt there could be no other Tooru.

"I, I…"

"I know it might be hard right away. But I still want to step into the shoes of the Kamiya that you cared about. I thought I didn't have anything to offer, but now I have something that lets me say with certainty, 'This is me.'"

I wondered if he was talking about the prize. His eyes brimmed with confidence. I could tell he didn't doubt himself in the slightest.

"When it comes to liking you, no one can beat me," he went on. "I'm confident I could have even beaten Kamiya. I realized that when I was working on my photo for the contest. That was the thing I really wanted, the thing that no one else has."

My chest ached. No one had ever liked me this much. No matter how much I liked Tooru, he loved Maori, and my own feelings were unrequited.

"But…I still like Kamiya…Tooru. I know he's gone now. I know I need to forget him. But it's too painful to do right away."

"Why do you need to forget him?"

"What?"

"You don't want to forget him, do you?"

"No, but I, I…have to forget him."

"No you don't. There's no reason to force yourself. Actually, it's better if you don't. After all—"

No reason to force myself to forget someone I couldn't forget. His words struck me. He smiled even more kindly.

"After all…you loved him."

My thoughts ceased, and everything went white. Endless white, or perhaps clarity, and in that blank space, I saw Tooru's smile. What did Naruse just say? That I loved Tooru?

"You loved him, didn't you? You cared more about him than about yourself. You're still suffering from his death. But I don't think you need to suffer. I'm sorry if I sound full of myself. He died, but he's still there inside you."

I didn't understand the meaning behind words about love. I couldn't believe in anything I hadn't felt. Things I hadn't felt didn't exist. Those words were mere expressions. I'd believed that until now. After all, I didn't think my own life had anything to do with them.

But maybe I was wrong. What if they were part of my life after all? I remembered what I had discovered that day in high school. I cared about Maori. I cared about Tooru. I cared about the two of them, and I wanted to put both of them before myself. That was the only pure, beautiful thing in me.

Now I realized there was a name for it. Naruse had just told me. The word settled naturally into my heart. When I reached toward it, the warmth spread. Tooru's figure rose silently within my mind. I smiled. I smiled as I cried. Something fell into place, and I finally understood.

I loved Tooru.

So that's what it was. It was all so simple. Why hadn't I realized something so obvious, it was staring me in the face?

I thought I had been suffering from a broken heart. You had to get over a broken heart. You couldn't let it hold you captive forever. But I was wrong. I was suffering because I had lost the person I loved. Of course it was painful. I loved him with my whole heart and soul. He meant more to me than myself. I couldn't stop crying. He was unbearably dear to me. I loved him. I loved him more deeply than anyone else. I didn't need to forget that feeling or that person just because he had died.

"I...don't have to forget Tooru," I mumbled, not wiping away my tears.

"No, you don't."

"You're not lying, right?"

"I'm not lying."

"I never got what I really wanted. If I did, I lost it right away. My loving parents, my first crush, the happiness of the people closest to me... But this is all right, isn't it? To keep my love for Tooru and not let it go? I can, can't I?"

"Yes, you can. Isn't it obvious?"

I couldn't help but feel like a child as his words put me at ease. Sense of security was another thing I thought I had lost. I had lost it as a child, and then when Tooru died, it had slipped through my fingers again, and I thought I would never get it back. But that wasn't true. Life didn't just take; it also gave. New friends, feelings, love. All of these things could be taken away but also given. When I looked at it that way, I saw my life filled with beautiful things. When I realized that, my face crumpled like a little child's.

I hadn't been able to show this face to my absent father, or to Tooru, who I loved. My true self, in all my weakness.

Dedicated to My Love

Time blurs people. Even things we promise never to forget fade with time. But so do the pains and sorrows we thought wouldn't ever disappear. Amid all of that, one thing never blurs and is instead carved indelibly into my mind.

On a day just after summer break ended, I was sitting on a bench behind the library, escaping from the hot sun. Even in this shady corner of the campus, people came and went in the morning rush. People who hadn't seen each other over the break met again with excited voices as they walked along the path in front of me. As I watched them, I heard someone running toward me. The nostalgic sound stopped nearby.

"Good morning, Wataya."

I hadn't seen that face all year. Naruse was smiling as he greeted me.

"Good morning, Naruse. Looks like it's gonna be another hot day."

"It does. It's so hot, I decided to buy some ice cream at the convenience store."

"Nice. What kind do you like?"

"I'd have to go with the ones shaped like a soft-serve cone."

As we chatted like we'd just seen each other the day before, some more people walked by.

"Hey, Naruse, you're back!"

They seemed to be friends of his. He looked up and said hello. They walked over to him.

"You look kind of different," one of them said.

"Hmm? Oh, I'm not sure. I might have gained some muscle. I was doing a lot of heavy lifting."

"Heavy lifting? Is everything all right now?"

"Yeah, thankfully. I got all the paperwork in; I'm back at school starting today."

I could tell they were treading carefully for his sake, and he smiled in response. He hadn't told his university friends what he'd been doing for the past year. Since he'd won the prize under the name Tooru Kamiya, they didn't know it was him, and they probably couldn't imagine it in their wildest dreams. But I knew. I knew what he'd been doing for the last year. I knew what he'd gained.

"Is it okay if I don't give you an answer right away?" I'd asked him that day after the award ceremony when he told me again how he felt. To my embarrassment, I'd cried in front of him, and I was far from gathering my own thoughts. But I promised that I would eventually give him an answer.

"That's no problem. I'll wait as long as it takes."

The next day, I met Tooru's sister at a café downtown. I told her about my conversation with Naruse after the party and everything that had led up to it. I also told her how he felt about me.

"I never imagined you'd be boasting to me one day about your love life!" she said with a smile, setting her cup of black tea down.

"Boasting? I didn't mean for it to sound like that."

"I was joking."

"...Oh."

We smiled amiably at each other. I could never have imagined this right after Tooru's death. If I could have seen into the future to this scene, I know I would have been dumbfounded.

"Anyway, I...well, I decided not to force myself to forget Tooru."

I described to her how my feelings toward Tooru had changed. I felt embarrassed, but I knew I could tell his sister anything. I wanted her to know.

"It seems you've discovered something important," she said kindly when I was done. Smiling softly, she went on. "To me, sadness was something to forget. All I knew how to do was forget it. But you've found something new within your sadness, haven't you?"

"It's nothing so praiseworthy as that. It's just...I cared so much about Tooru, and it's like I realized how much I did. I realized that even after he died, I didn't stop caring for him, that my feelings didn't change."

Maybe I had been at a loss about what to do with my feelings for the person I loved after he died. But I didn't need to get rid of them or to grieve their loss. They were still here. Something that exists does not disappear. I simply needed to acknowledge it and value it.

Maybe what I was saying sounded childish to Tooru's sister. Nevertheless, she listened intently.

"If you wrote a novel now, you might end up with something different."

"Different?"

"Yes. In a way, novels reflect how the person writing them sees the world. Although there is a limit to the types of stories that can exist, there is no limit to the perspectives a person can have of the world. I call it style, and as long as there is style, there will be an endless supply of the kind of novels you and I like."

I listened in a daze. His sister gave her beautiful, infinitely elegant smile.

"Within that world, what kind of novel will you write?"

That evening, I returned to the city where I lived. I spent the rest of summer vacation quietly, thinking over many things. When the fall semester began, Naruse returned to school. He greeted me as if nothing had happened. I replied as usual. He had many friends, and lots of people were happy to see him back at the university.

Once again, he became a part of my daily life. Our mutual friend invited me to go out to the pub with a few friends to celebrate his return. He didn't act flustered around me. He smiled calmly, gently. Sometimes, he had his camera around his neck. He seemed to love that camera. When he took pictures around campus, people he knew would come up to him. They would talk a little, and then he would take their picture. In front of him, everyone smiled.

"Hello, Wataya!"

As I watched him at work, he caught sight of me. After thanking the people he'd been photographing, he ran over to me.

"You don't have to run."

"I was happy to see you."

"I swear you—"

As we talked, I noticed something. I brought my hand to my cheek.

"What is it, Wataya? Did I say something funny?"

I shook my head, still smiling as I reassured him that it was nothing.

The day I had tea in Tokyo with Tooru's sister, she'd told me something at the end of our conversation.

"By the way, back when Tooru was alive…"

Before she received the Akutagawa Prize, she and Tooru met by chance at the bookstore where she was doing a signing. It was the day Tooru had planned to go to the aquarium with me and Maori, but instead he went to talk with his sister and asked me to explain his absence to her. His sister said that was when he told her he had found someone he liked, a girl named Maori. When she told him to treat her the best he could, he said, "I will. And I won't just treat her well. I'll do everything I can to be that kind of person."

To be that kind of person…

I couldn't help feeling deeply impressed. Tooru really had been just that. Just about anyone can temporarily treat another person kindly. But life goes on. Things happen that prevent us from treasuring the things we had thought we wanted to value. Everything keeps moving forward, with such miserable, merciless inevitability that it makes you sad. Yet Tooru was not a temporary presence. He devoted his whole life to treating Maori well. He became that kind of person. Maybe that was why he asked me to erase him from her mind if anything happened to him.

As I thought back on it as a university student, I felt that I, too, wanted to be like that. Would I be able to, though? Could I value someone that much, treat them that well? Could I find someone other than Tooru to be that way with?

…Maybe I had already found them.

Summer changed to fall, and I still hadn't given Naruse a clear answer. One day as I was sitting on a bench on campus between interviews for a postgraduation job, he walked up to me.

"Hello, Wataya," he said. As usual, he had found me in a spot that people rarely frequented and come to say hello. He asked if he could sit down next to me, and I nodded. We chatted for a few minutes, then looked up at the sky together.

"People in your year are starting to get serious about finding jobs, right?"

"You'll be doing the same before you know it. What's your plan? Will you pursue photography?"

"Instead of that, I think I want to do something behind the scenes to support photographers. I feel like that would be a better fit."

Despite the prize, he didn't seem interested in becoming a professional. He said he was continuing to take photos as a hobby, and he told me about his mentor, Sakurai. I'd heard him talk about Sakurai before. He seemed like an eccentric person, but a nice one.

"I bet from your perspective, everyone seems like a good person," I said.

"Maybe you're right. I'm a happy-go-lucky guy."

He smiled. As usual, his camera was around his neck. I looked at it silently. It wasn't so much that I momentarily forgot my doubts and reticence but that they didn't exist anymore.

"Hey, how about taking my picture with that?" I said. He was dumbfounded.

"What? No, I couldn't!"

"Why not?"

"...Okay, fine."

He took pictures of his friends all the time, but he'd never tried to take one of me. I'd never asked him to. He stood up from the bench, looking a little nervous. He walked around, searching for the right angle and finally, with a serious expression, held the camera to his eye.

"Tell me before you take it, okay?"

"Oh, okay. So...I'm gonna take it."

The next instant, I heard the sound of the shutter. I opened up to him. There in a place where I felt safe, I smiled from the bottom of my heart.

When he was done taking pictures, he looked dazed. He checked the photos, then looked up at me in surprise. I stood and walked over to him. "It's chilly, isn't it?" I said, and took his hand.

More than a year earlier, when we went on a date at the aquarium, we had held hands, and I thought his had felt frail. But now it felt big and rough.

"By the way, I'll go out with you," I said quietly. He widened his eyes slightly. "But I have one condition."

I gave him a teasing look, and he grinned. "And what is it?" he asked.

"You can fall in love with me because I'll fall in love with you. I'm already starting to. But in exchange, you have to promise me one thing."

I smiled at him as I remembered all the people I had parted with and met in my life.

"You absolutely must live longer than me."

The smile vanished from his face, and as if he took a deep breath, his expression grew serious. I turned toward him and tried to continue, but I was shaking. I made myself open my mouth.

"I know full well that it's enough for someone to live on in my heart. But, and maybe this sounds obvious, if they're alive, it's even better. It's much more joyful. So I'm begging you. Please don't die before me. Let me treasure you for a long, long time."

That was my one wish, and my one condition. That he didn't die before me.

Maybe he would think it was a selfish request. And maybe it was impossible to guarantee something like that. But I wanted him to promise. I wanted him to take care of his own life.

Please don't leave the person who smiles at you with all her heart, the person who loves you. Please don't leave me alone.

My face must have looked horrible from trying so hard to hold back my tears. I couldn't look him in the face because I didn't want him to see me like that. But he still heard what I was saying. He gently squeezed my hand.

"Starting today, I will eat lots of vegetables," he said.

Reflexively, I looked at him. His expression was solemn.

"I will work out whether I like it or not. I will strive to eat fish rather than red meat. I will be careful about my salt intake."

The contrast between his words and his face was so funny, I almost burst out laughing. He was even himself at a moment like this. Innocent and serious and...

"I will never leave you alone. Never ever."

Sincere to the tips of his toes. Although I was aware of the pain deep in my eyes, I smiled at him.

"Make sure you also get your yearly checkup," I joked. He smiled gently.

"I promise," he answered. Then he wrapped his arms around me like he was holding something very important to him.

This is the end of the story of my first love and how I found someone new. Meeting Maori and the two Toorus has made up for all the tears and sadness in my life.

When Naruse hugged me, I was overwhelmed by tenderness and kissed his cheek. As I did, I was reminded of a day in the past. Tooru's wake was held in spring after our third year of high school ended. When it was Maori's turn to offer a stick of incense, she looked silently at Tooru lying in his coffin. After the service ended, she began to feel unwell. She staggered and became faint. Worried, Tooru's sister and father brought her to a quiet room to rest. I was worried, too, and went with them, but thinking her family should come get her, I left the room.

I found a place where she wouldn't be able to overhear the conversation and called her mother. She answered right away and said she would come get Maori. I had intended to go straight back to her, but a thought crossed my mind.

I wanted to be with Tooru one more time.

Maybe he had already been moved. Maybe I wouldn't be able to go into the room where the wake had been held. But when I got to the lamplit hall, it wasn't locked.

Tooru was still there.

No, it was only his body. His soul wasn't there. He had already left on his journey to the next world. The entity that had been Tooru had vanished like smoke, and it could never return to his body. All the same, I walked toward the first boy I had ever liked.

He lay inside the coffin with his eyes closed. His face had always been pale, but now it was even paler. Deep affection welled up within me. I wanted to touch him. Without thinking, I placed my hand on his cheek. On the day of the school festival, my lips had brushed that cheek. That time, it had been unintentional, a coincidence. But this time…

I felt guilty toward Maori, but I couldn't stop myself.

I'll carry out his last wish. I'll prevent Maori from knowing about his death. I'll do everything after that, everything. I'll protect her. So…please.

Imploring forgiveness from someone, anyone, I softly placed my lips against his cheek.

Remembering the day I said goodbye to the person I loved, I slowly opened my eyes. Naruse was smiling bashfully. The day of the wake, Tooru's cheek had been heartbreakingly cold when I kissed it. The person I loved had turned cold as stone. He would never move, never open his eyes. I had never dreamed something like that would happen.

Now I was touching something warm. I felt the warmth of the person I currently loved, and the person I had loved before. The warmth was there and real, and I wanted to believe in it.

A tear streamed down my face, just like it had when I kissed Tooru's cheek. It, too, was warm.

Naruse and I became a couple, and I remained close friends with Maori. After she entered university, she continued to desperately try to remember Tooru. But that didn't mean she neglected her present-day life. She enjoyed herself and broadened her horizons, but she also chose to continue trying to remember Tooru.

I was putting more energy into my job search while also continuing to write my novel. Naruse had reached his goal, but I was still striving for mine. I swore that one day, my novel would reach Tooru's sister. When I looked into the work I submitted for the contest, I discovered that it had been rejected in the second round. The novel I submitted in my junior year of university made it to the third round. By the time I learned the results, I was done with my job search. The following spring, I would graduate from university and begin work right away.

That year passed in a flash. The second spring after graduating, I went with Maori to view the cherry blossoms. I had continued seeing her after I started my new job. She was a senior in college now, the same as Naruse since he had taken a year off.

Maori was still trying to remember Tooru. Using her journals and my descriptions, she went to the places they had visited, did the things they had done, and desperately tried to remember him. By continuing to delve into her own mind in this way, she gradually began to succeed.

At her invitation, we gazed at the blossoms, talked happily, and walked through the park between the rows of cherry trees. It was the park where she and Tooru had gone on their first date and where the three of us had visited in high school. While we were there, I realized something. I closed my eyes and tried to recall an image of Tooru. He appeared there in the darkness, but his face was slightly hazy. It made me sad to realize he was fading into the past.

I had wanted so badly to forget him, and I had cried when I realized it was all right not to. Time mercilessly marches on, pulling everything into its orbit. It turned everything into the past. No one can stop time or resist oblivion.

But even so, people…hold on to things. They don't forget what is important to them. When I talked about Tooru, Maori remembered something new about him. She began to draw him in her sketchbook.

"I loved him…and he's gone. But the memories are here inside me. Sleeping here in my body and heart. By remembering him, we can continue to live together; I can't explain it very well, but it's similar to hope. The world is gradually forgetting him. But…"

Maori looked inward and drew a Tooru not recorded in any photograph or video. As I watched her draw, I was deeply moved. She drew Tooru with her heart, turning her vision of him into a drawing that would remain over time. I couldn't do that. But I had my own way of keeping him with us that only I could do. After we walked in the park, I went home and began writing a new novel. I had just submitted one to a contest in February, but I had an overwhelming urge to write a new one. I felt like I had to write it.

I drew Tooru with my words, in my own style. That was something only I could do. The next year, I submitted that novel as my fifth entry to the writing contest and won an award. It took five years, but I achieved my goal of having Tooru's sister read my novel.

Naruse got a job with a camera manufacturer. He was happy when

I told him I'd won. We're still together. I have his picture *Last Ice* on my phone. Naruse had continued taking pictures in his free time, and he introduced me to his friend and mentor, Sakurai. They get along as well as two little kids and see each other often.

I wasn't sure if I should tell Maori about the literature prize. I decided to wait until it was published. I wondered how she would react when she found out I was a novelist. Would she be happy for me?

After the awards ceremony that summer, I began the work needed to publish it. With advice from my editor and Tooru's sister, I revised and added more to the novel. It was hard to do while working full time, but I enjoyed it. On a fall day, beneath a broad blue sky, I finished the revisions. All that remained was to send the file to my editor for a final review. After I saved the file, I scrolled up to the top page. I gazed silently at the screen. I still had one more thing to do.

I hadn't talked to my editor about it, but I added an extra blank page. I began to type in the center of the page. *I dedicate this book to Tooru Kamiya, who is no longer with us.* I stared at the blinking cursor. My editor would probably let me get away with that much, but I bet they would make me delete the next line. That was fine. To me, this was the complete version of the novel.

I kept typing. I would continue to remember Tooru in my own way. I would not hand him over to the past, to oblivion. Never. He was my one and only first love. My one and only heartbreak. My wound. My pain. My tears. All of it was a treasure to me. A glittering, beautiful thing. Without meaning to, I remembered him, and my eyes stung. How many days and months had passed since he died? Maybe life is fleeting. Once lit, our fire is fated to go out. No one can escape that.

But when people go, they leave something warm behind. I still feel warmth from the glow of his life. Tooru isn't in this world anymore, but he exists inside me. There was something I wanted to say to him. He isn't in the world we can see with our eyes, but I wanted to say it to the Tooru who was within me.

You lived a beautiful life.

I want to tell you that you lived with kindness and warmth, more beautifully than anyone I know.

I typed the final words. As I read the sentence I had just written, I smiled at its inadequacy. Still, I had finally given him shape. Given shape to Tooru...

I dedicate this book to Tooru Kamiya,
who is no longer with us.
With friendship, respect, and incomparable love.

Afterword

Sometimes I think about things that used to exist inside me, and things that have disappeared. Passion for certain things, habits, and feelings toward people. If they vanished naturally, I am able to tell myself logically that maybe I no longer needed them. But not everything disappears like that. Some things disappear even when we don't want them to because the environment has changed, or the object of a certain feeling has been lost. Single-minded passion, habits we are attached to, feelings toward others.

How should we respond when we are forced to give up things we had wanted very much to keep? This book is about a young woman who loses someone she loves. It is also the story of her discovering beautiful emotions within herself even as she loses something she cared about more than herself.

As long as we are alive, no matter how peaceful our lives, we cannot remain without wounds. Still, even if we lose something important, I believe that we don't also need to lose the love we had for that thing or our desire to hold it dear. Things that we think we have lost can remain in other forms.

The remainder of this afterword is acknowledgments.

This book is a spinoff of *Even If This Love Disappears Tonight* and a story I had wanted to write from the time I was working on that book. I am very happy that thanks to the support from many people, I had the opportunity to send it out into the world.

As a result, I've been with my editor for a bit longer. I hope we continue to work together in the future.

To everyone who was involved in the movie adaption of the book, I would like to acknowledge that the reason I was able to publish Izumi Wataya's story is thanks to your hard work on the film. I am deeply grateful.

To Koichi, who designed the cover, thank you for creating another beautiful book. Since it is difficult to meet in person right now, please let me express my appreciation here. I first encountered your work on the day of the awards ceremony for the 26th Dengeki Novel Prize, about an hour before it began. The editor in charge of covers for the winning manuscripts showed me some samples, and I remember very well that I told them I wanted you to design my cover. Ever since, my books have included your photographs. You handled the cover for my second book as well, and fortunately both have been translated and published abroad. You express the outlook of the world within the story in a single photograph and capture the crucial moments and emotions. You make people smile. Through knowing you, I have become aware of the many powers of photography, and that became one of the themes in this book. I truly look forward to the day I have the opportunity to thank you in person.

Finally, let me thank all the readers. Although the following words may be clichéd, the feeling of gratitude is always new. Thank you so much for picking up this book. Since I cannot thank each of you individually, please let me once again bow in appreciation to you through these words. May we meet again one day.

MISAKI ICHIJO

Even If This Love Disappears Tonight

Misaki Ichijo

Even If This Love Disappears Tonight
Misaki Ichijo

I fell in love with you whose memories disappear after a day, a love that will never come again.

When Tooru Kamiya is pushed into falsely confessing his love to Maori Hino, she tells him they can date on the condition he doesn't truly fall in love with her. To his surprise, Tooru agrees. However, as they become closer, he finds that he cannot adhere to it anymore. When he finally tells her how he feels, Maori reveals that she has an illness—she's unable to remember anything that happened the day before. Nevertheless, Tooru is determined to build a relationship with her one day at a time…